MW00966060

LOVING EYES
CAN'T
SEE

To: Mrs. Bowser;
To a very sweet lady"
God Bless!
Penny Glover
"2010"

LOVING EYES CAN'T SEE

A NOVEL BY PENNY GLOVER

© COPYRIGHTED 2009 PENNY GLOVER

ISBN 978-0-557-32244-2

The novel, "Loving Eye's Can't See," is about Domestic Violence. There may be some material in this novel that may make you wonder how could one live with themselves doing the things that they do to other people. How one can be so heartless. I will give you a young girl's view of the world, to a young man's view. That is why I am telling you both sides of the story to make a point, and the way their two different worlds intertwined. One grew up with lots of love, and the other grew up with plenty of hate. It's sad but true. Taliyah Loving Masterson just happened to be caught up in both worlds. It's too bad that she found out so late about the people that she thought she could trust with her life...

**This book is dedicated to my mother,
"Mrs. Bettie R. Glover"
"Love You Forever"**

*Father please lead me the way through the
obstacles that I am challenged with each day.*

Acknowledgements

First and foremost, I would like to thank God, the Father Almighty for blessing me with the gift of the imagination that I definitely have. All I have to do is sit in front of my computer staring at a blank page and the characters just come to me. Then I would like to thank my biological family for supporting me and edging me on when I would start slacking down on my writing, to my co-workers, who are also my family for I am with them more than any other place, and to my church family, who I look to for spiritual guidance. You all play an important role in my life and I want to thank you. Love you all, and mean it.

Contents

CHAPTER 1

Flat lined. That's right. The doctor just told my family that I have just passed. I am not breathing anymore. There is nothing else that can be done. I'm dead. Yes, this is something that's going to happen to everyone and everything that breathes, for no one, or thing lives forever.

If only you could see my family right now. Everyone is hollering and crying in disbelief as if they are surprised that they didn't see it coming. I'm not even a psychic and knew eventually that this would happen. Just not to the extent that it happened.

Wow, who knew that I could see and hear everything that's going on around me? Oh-oo, I'm going to miss this life. I'm really going to miss my Aunt Maxine, my mother's sister. She was my heart. I loved her to death.

(No pun intended) She is the one who taught me about life and men in general, for she had plenty of them. Towards the end of my journey on earth, she tried her best to help me, but I was too far gone. There wasn't anything that could be said to me. I wouldn't listen to anybody for I knew that I could handle the situation that I had ended up in. I guess you know by now that I was wrong.

I had been playing Russian roulette for quite some time with my life. The reason for all of this is because of that dangerous word called Love. That's right, I said it. Love is a dangerous word. Well, at least that is what I think of it in my mind now. When you hear the saying, "Love Don't Love Nobody," believe me, nothing could be more truthful. I know what you're thinking right now. That you love yourself so much that no one can take advantage of you right? That you've got yourself together, and that only people with low self-esteem have the problem of letting someone manipulate them. No one can get to you.

Well, I'm lying here getting colder by the minute as the new falling snow to tell you that I thought I knew and had it all too. Talking about being shit on a stick. Humph, I thought my shit didn't stink. Who me? Yea right. Not until I had someone actually put my face in my own shit that I knew it that it stank. You read it right. Gross isn't it? Well brace yourself for that was the least of my problems.

I've been called a Bitch so many times, that one day I was told by a woman that I saw in a mall that if someone ever called me a Bitch again, to just brush it off and keep doing what I'm doing. Believe me, I did. They broke it down to me with each letter and said that a Bitch meant a woman "Being In Total Control of Herself."

That woman only had to tell me that just once for I've never forgotten it. I walked around with that motto being a Diva and all. Yes a DIVA. That meant to me as to be Dignified, Independent, Versatile, Arrogant, and Attractive. I am a DIVA-A.

Hello. Let me introduce myself. My name is Taliyah Loving Masterson. I will describe myself to you as no one else can. I am five feet seven inches tall, 125 pounds, with light hazel eyes and naturally curly hair, in which I would always swing around when I would see a woman who didn't have any. If a woman was with her boyfriend, of course I would do it. I didn't need the attention at all for I was getting that anyway. I did it because I could. Sometimes the woman would call me all kinds of Bitches in which I would just laugh it off and walk away. Depending on where I was, I would step into my baby blue convertible Mercedes sports car, wink at the boyfriend as I put on my sunshades, and then drive away. Remember the commercial with the woman saying that to not hate her for being beautiful? That was me all the way. Ever since I was born, that was all I heard, no matter where my parents took me. It was instilled in me from day one.

Humph, I thought that I was so fine, that when I walked into a room full of people, that either they wanted to be with me, take a picture of me, or wanted to be me. That's how arrogant I was. If I may say so myself, and you know that I will, it definitely wasn't a lie. Let the truth be told. Every time I would pass a mirror, (which was often) I would blow a kiss at myself and smile. There was no need to touch-up my makeup, for it was done for me by my friend Gregory. I felt that the world needed me. For without me who would anyone look up to by me being so beautiful? Like I said before, don't hate.

All of that came to a halt when I met a mind blowing, man named Martell Chancellor Harrington. "Chance" as he was called. He was a fine specimen of a man if there ever was one. He was so fine that he made me stop in my tracks. Now that usually doesn't happen. It was I that was the one who men and women would fawn over. This was something new to me. Of course, I tried to keep my Diva cool at the time. I don't know what happened. He made a feeling come through my body that I've never felt before. Now that was powerful. It was those piercing dark eyes that were looking at me that seemed to be tearing my clothes off piece by piece. (It could have been that I was horny as hell too) It didn't take much for me to get turned on by men of power. All of a sudden, I got hot and had to go to the restroom to cool myself off. As I was walking out, he was right there, and offered to buy me a drink as he introduced himself. Of course, I said yes, no doubt about it. This was the beginning of one of my worst nightmares....

CHAPTER 2

(The Beginning)

"Push baby push! You can do it!"

"Oooh! It hurts so badly! Woo-woo-woo!!"

"That's right, keep pushing. The baby is coming. Just give it one more big push and she'll be here," says the doctor.

"Oooh! Oooh! Woo-woo-woo! Oh God, please help me!!" cries Brooke. Please take it out! Take it out!!

"Here she comes! Her head is coming out! Just give it one more big push and she will be out" says the doctor.

"That's right baby. Give it one more push," says Marvin her husband.

"Shut up!! Shouts Brooke. "If it weren't for you, I wouldn't be in this position!!"

"Calm down baby," says Marvin knowing that she didn't mean what she said.

"Here she comes! Here she is a lovely baby girl!" says the doctor. All of a sudden a loud cry comes from the baby that lets everyone know that she is here.

"She has finally decided to come," says Marvin.

"Ms. Taliyah Loving Masterson. That will be her name," says Brooke. The nurse takes the baby, washes her off, and then gives her to Brooke.

"She is so beautiful," says Brooke.

"That's my baby. She is perfect, and is going to have the world served to her on a silver platter. Whatever Loving wants, Loving will get," says Marvin.

✳ From then on, that is the way it has been. Taliyah Loving Masterson has gotten whatever she wanted. No matter what it took, her every wish was granted.

As Loving grew up, she never had to make up her bed, or fix her own breakfast in the mornings before she went off to private school. She only had the best of everything. Even though it seemed that she was the only child because her brother was sent off to boarding school. They rarely saw each other only on visits at holidays and special occasions.

It was on Thanksgiving that Morgan came home from school for good. Loving hardly knew him because of the distance between them. She had only seen pictures of him lately and would talk to him over the phone.

When Morgan walked in the door, Loving couldn't believe her eyes. He was just as handsome as ever. In fact, he looked almost exactly like her, but in male form. Morgan is a couple of years older than Loving and when he walks towards her to embrace her, she feels a strange feeling come over her. There is a warm presence about him.

"Hey sis, stand back. I want to take a good look at you. You're beautiful. I know that I have a big job ahead of me trying to keep all the men off of you. You have your big brother here now protecting his little sis." Loving smiles and says, "Let me introduce you to my best friend Gregory. While you were gone he was my protector."

"Are you sure that was all it was?" asks Morgan.

"Believe me, I'm sure." She calls Gregory over to her and says, "Gregory, this is my big brother Morgan.

"Oh, is he really? It's so nice to finally meet you," says Gregory as he scans Morgan up and down and thinking to himself what he could do and for Morgan while all the time smiling.

"Thank you for looking after my sister. I appreciate it."

"My pleasure," says Gregory. "My pleasure," he says, as he stares into Morgan's eyes. Loving notices the stares and says, "Well, we're finally going to get to sit down and have a decent conversation face to face."

"We have a lot to catch up on being that I've been away from the family for so long. Now that I'm back, we can get to know each other much better as brothers and sisters should," says Morgan.

"That's what I like to hear," says their aunt Maxine as she walks in on them as they are talking. "M-m-m, you smell so good," says Maxine as she hugs Morgan real tight and gives him a kiss on the cheek. "Stand back so that I can take a good look at you. Looking just like your sister. You two could go for twins."

"Loving looks like me. I'm the oldest remember?"

"Oh, alright then," says Maxine as she takes him by the hand and sashays into the den where her husband David and the rest of the company are. "Honey, this is my nephew Morgan. He has just come home from school and we will be seeing him quite a bit now that he has decided to stay closer to home."

"Hey man. How you doing? It's nice to meet you. You can hang around here with the men or whatever. Just make yourself comfortable.

"Thanks. I think I might just do that," says Morgan as he notices someone that he may be interested in.

"Talking about apples not falling far from the tree, says Gregory.

"What do you mean by that?" Loving asks.

"Look at your brother. He's just as high maintenance as you are, and I love it."

"There you go trying to get to my brother before he's in the door good."

"What better time than that. What do you want me to do? Wait for the little bitches to come swarming around him? I'm just like time baby. I wait for nothing or no one. The time is now or else," says Gregory.

"Or else you'll do what? I think that you had better cool yourself down Diva. Do you remember someone by the name of Christopher? The person that you're already involved with? In fact, the one who is actually in the other room? You know how crazy he is about you. I know that you're not going to hurt him because you can't keep your hormones in check. Anyway, you just met my brother a few minutes ago. I don't even know how he really is yet myself."

"You didn't have to break it down like that. Yes I do remember who Christopher is, and can't I have some kind of fantasy? Humph, if the time and place is right, that fantasy is going to end up being a reality."

"So what you're trying to say is that my brother's gay?" asks Loving."

"I'm not trying to say anything. You can take it any way you want to. Like I said before, if the timing is right, there could be some sparks flying that's all."

"The only sparks that's going to fly is when Morgan knocks you out for stepping out of bounds with him. It will be sparks, but not the kind that you would like," says Loving.

"We'll see about that," says Gregory.

"Why are you so head strong on trying to seduce my brother? Is it because he is new in town, and you want to be the first one to try him out?"

"No, but I know what I know," says Gregory.

"Just don't come to me when he beats the crap out of you for trying to come on to him."

"Don't worry about me. I know how to take care of myself," says Gregory.

"Speaking of high maintenance, where is my mother? I haven't seen her in awhile. I know that she isn't cooking," says Loving.

"Here she comes now. Hello Mrs. Masterson. Happy Thanksgiving," says Gregory.

"Happy Thanksgiving baby, how's your Mom doing?"

"She's doing pretty good. Thanks for asking."

"Tell her to give me a call so that we can have lunch sometime soon."

"I sure will."

Meanwhile, Morgan walks over to where Maxine is talking to some young ladies to say hello. They all turn around and Maxine puts her hand on Morgan's shoulder and says, "Ladies, this is Morgan, my nephew and Loving's brother. He has just come from school and will be sticking around this time. Morgan makes eye contact with one lady in particular and she says, "Hello Morgan, my name is Courtney, a good friend of Loving."

"It's nice to meet you Courtney" he says. Maxine tells him that Courtney is a good friend of the family. Courtney has been around our family since she was knee-high, and is at every function that we have. We made her part of the family."

"Part of the family huh? I guess that I will be seeing you quite a bit now that I'll be around."

"Anytime that you want," says Courtney.

"I just might take you up on that," says Morgan.

"This is Paige and Autumn" says Maxine. These girls all grew up with Loving. Morgan looks at Autumn who has light brown hair that reminds him of the leaves that changes color for the season.

"We are right in the middle of your season. One of the best seasons of them all in my opinion," says Morgan as he looks into her eyes.

"I agree," says Autumn now smiling. She starts to get weak in the knees as she gazes back at him.

"Hello Paige. What a pretty name for a pretty lady," says Morgan.

"Thank-you," smiles Paige. She is the one that Morgan was looking at when he first walked into the room.

"Nice to meet you all, and I'm sorry to cut this short, but I have a habit that is hard to break. I have to go and take a smoke right now. I'm sure that I will get to talk to each one of you later. Before I leave, I would like to know who that young man is that is standing over there"

"That's Christopher, Gregory's friend," says Maxine.

"Okay." He takes a mental note to introduce himself after he comes back from outside. He then walks out towards the door to have a smoke.

Around a half hour later, Maxine calls everyone for dinner. "There's plenty to eat and drink, so enjoy yourselves."

"Good, for I'm famished," says Loving as she and Gregory go to the table to sit down to eat. Christopher comes in the room with Morgan and sits down beside him.

Everyone is seated at the table and Maxine prays over the food. As she is praying, her brother-in-law Levy who has been drinking since he's been at the house says, "Can somebody please help her say the prayer, because I don't think that she knows what she's doing. I'm about to fall asleep right here at the table if she doesn't stop soon. Blah, Blah, Blah."

Maxine gives him a stern look, and then says, "Amen." Everyone else says, "Amen."

David doesn't say anything to his brother until everyone has finished eating and has left the table. He then takes his brother outside and lays him out for disrespecting his wife and his home the way he did. David then tells Levy to stay outside until he gets himself together. The fresh air might do him some good.

"Aw-w-w man, I didn't mean any harm. I was just trying to add a little humor to the situation that's all."

"A little humor? My wife was praying in there and you say it was just a little humor? Man, you had better get your act together, or the next time you will not be invited to my home again. You hear me?"

"I still don't know what the big deal is. It's not like she's Mother Teresa or somebody. (David gives Levy a look that says, man, watch yourself) What? Nobody can say anything to her without you coming to the rescue?"

'You don't get it do you? My wife was praying. I'm wasting my time standing here talking to your drunk ass. I tell you what. Stay away from my home until you can give me the respect that I give your wife okay?" David then walks away from him back into the house and slams the door behind him.

While they were talking, unbeknownst to them, Courtney, who is standing outside by the garage smoking is watching them. When David goes back into the house, she walks over to Levy and asks him if he is okay.

"Hell no, I'm not okay" he says.

"I saw you and Mr. Cameron arguing and he went back into the house and slammed the door," says Courtney.

"Yea, my brother is always making something out of nothing. He has no sense of humor. He gets on my nerves being so serious all the time. I wish that he would loosen up sometimes. Why are you asking anyway? What can you do to help me?"

"Maybe I can give you a ride home or something."

"You can give me a ride alright, but not to my home. I know that you know my wife is in the house, and I guess you don't care. You can give me a ride on that big range that you have back there though."

"What? I'm sorry, but I don't know what you're talking about," says Courtney, surprised that he would say something like that.

"You know damn well what I'm talking about. I've noticed you before at other functions that the family had. You were always trying to get my attention. You definitely have my full attention now, and I'm saluting you at this very moment."

"Excuse me? I didn't come over here to be insulted by you. I was trying to help you."

"You can help me alright, by letting me kiss those big juicy lips of yours."

"I had better go now. You're getting way out of hand. Those people in that house are a part of my family too. Ms. Brooke is like a second mother to me. I cannot disrespect them like that.

"Why are you still standing here talking to me then? When I first said something out of the way you could have stopped me right then but you didn't. What about my wife? You haven't said a word about disrespecting her. Your ass is just as hot as burning coal right now. I can see the steam coming from under that dress that you have on.

Look at you. You haven't moved an inch. You know why? Because you want me to stick my hard log up in you, and stir that hot coal that's why." says Levy as he draws Courtney closer to him.

"I don't want to get into any trouble," says Courtney, (now breathing hard).

"You're not going to get into any trouble. Trouble is about to enter into you." Levy starts to sing, "Nothing could be finer, than a woman and her vagina." He takes Courtney by the hand and starts to dance. As he turns her around, he stops and kisses her lips and then sticks his tongue into her mouth. At first, Courtney tries to resist, but then she lets go and kisses him back. They only stop again to get into the back of Levy's car by the garage, a place where they both think that no one can see them because of the trees. Levy lifts up Courtney's dress and begins to caress her breasts. He puts one of her breasts into his mouth as Courtney leans back and enjoys the feeling and lets Levy get his way with her. As he penetrates himself inside of her she lets out a moan. He starts to get in motion with Courtney like a surfer on a big wave at the beach. They don't stop until they both come to a climax.

After they are through, Levy stays on top of Courtney as she tries her best to push him off of her when he falls asleep. She can't call for help, because she knows that she is wrong for being with Loving's uncle. Courtney keeps pushing on Levy until she finally rolls him off of her enough so that she can slide herself from under him. She then opens the car door and carefully lets herself out holding her dress in front of her. She hurries to get into her car and drives away. What she doesn't know is that someone has been watching them all the time.

Meanwhile, back at the house, Elaine, Levy's wife, is upset that he has shown off again and apologizes to Maxine and David.

"There's no need to keep apologizing for him. Levy is a grown man. He knows what he's doing," says David.

"I know, but don't you think that you were just a little too hard on him this time? Nobody's perfect."

"I never said that they were. It's just that he's not going to keep coming over here and disrespecting my family. Why don't you give him a little more attention at home?" asks David.

"What do you mean?" asks Elaine.

"That wasn't a hard question," says David.

"What does that have to do with anything with me not giving him enough attention at home?"

"Yes it does. It seems to me every time the family has something Levy is the one that shows his ass," says David.

"As you said before, Levy is a grown man, and even though I'm his wife, I can't control everything that he does. You should know that yourself. I'm sure that you being perfect and all can't even imagine doing anything wrong," says Elaine now trying to hold back tears.

"Now you're talking crazy, for nobody's perfect. What broke the camel's back is when Maxine was praying, and he is joking around. What kind of person is that? He is not allowed in my house until he apologizes to my wife and family," says David.

"That was rather rude of him Elaine. Being that I was praying," says Maxine.

"I know. I was there. You don't have to keep emphasizing that okay? If my husband is not welcome here, I'm not either," says Elaine tearfully.

"Wait a minute. No need for you to get mad at me for something that your dumb ass husband did."

"Why does he have to be called names? He had a little too much to drink before he got here, and now you two have put him on the danger list."

"There you go, blowing everything out of proportion. Your problem is that you can't see the forest from the trees. He sat up there and embarrassed you too. You don't even have sense enough to know it," says Maxine.

"Wait a minute. Stop right there!" shouts Elaine. Before she finishes what she is saying, Morgan walks in.

"Excuse me, but are we going to discuss this all night, or are we going to finish celebrating? Look who I found outside sleeping in his car." It is Levy who has come to apologize. They all look at each other and laugh.

"We're here to celebrate. Now let's go and sit down and enjoy ourselves. They all go down to the basement where the music is playing and the rest of the family and guests are sitting around at the bar or dancing.

CHAPTER 3

(Chance)

Life is like being in an amusement park. When you walk in an amusement park for the first time, you are so excited, and want to see everything. Want to ride on the largest roller coasters. Go to the water rides, and have the thrill of getting wet all over. Loving every minute when the water splashes on you. Your clothes will be stuck to your skin until they dry, as you walk around the park. You don't care, because it is so hot, that it takes no time for them to dry. Anyway, you are having too much fun to care.

Then there's the food. All the different kinds of food that you can taste, from countries that you know you'll never visit. Knowing that you can imagine being in that country just by going into a certain location in the park. The funnel cakes are so delicious, that you keep going back to again and again. They are something that you don't get at home, and are a major part of enjoying yourself as you walk around the park eating. You try to decide which ride that you are going to get on next that will give you a bigger thrill as the roller coaster.

Yes, this is how life is. Just like a baby is born, he is curious, and wants to touch everything that he can get his hands on, and taste everything that he can get into his mouth. Not knowing that everything that is touched and tasted is not good for you. As we grow older, it doesn't change. We are still curious, and will get into things that may not seem bad at the time, but eventually that will catch up with you. As my grandmother used to say, "What feels or tastes good to you is not always good for you."

Yes, we all reap what we sow. What vibes are put out into the world by you, will come to you twofold whether positive or negative.

My name is Martell Chancellor Harrington, named after a father who only left me grief and scars for life, not only on my body, but on my spirit as well. He is one part of the reason I feel the way I do today towards women.

I am five feet eleven inches tall. A very attractive man, who doesn't have to do anything to attract a woman, women approach me. That's right. You see, they fall for the dimples, and the smooth sense of style every time. Once a woman gets involved with me, she is headed for a ride of her life. Just like the roller coaster. What she doesn't know is that I actually resent her. I resent all women. My mother made me the way I am.

When I was a baby, my mother used to put barrettes on my head because my hair was so long, and people would think that I was a little girl when she would take me out. She wanted to have a daughter so bad, that I was as close to a little girl as she could get to. You see, after I was born, she couldn't have any more kids because of the complications with me at birth. This made her go into a depression state.

As I got older, and started school, she was still doing it. I was teased a lot in school because of it. Not because of the hair itself, but because the way she would still put barrettes in my hair. One day, she decided in her warped mind to send me to school in a pink dress with tights, and black patent leather shoes. In fact, she walked me to school to make sure that I went. She took and seated me in the classroom. I cried and pleaded with my mother to please not leave me there, but she laughed it off along with the other kids who were in the class. When my mother left out of the class with the teacher, the boys in the room surrounded me, and started to pull up the dress that I was wearing and was pulling my hair. I was so humiliated and confused. It was a nightmare. How could my mother do this to her own son? When the teacher did come back into the classroom, (which seemed like years in my mind), she took me to the principal's office and called my father. My father did not know that my mother had been sending me to school that way. He had to get off of work to come pick me up from school. When we did get home, my father beat my mother so bad that day, she had to go to the hospital. No charges were filed, so there wasn't anything the police could do.

The reason that I'm telling you all this, is because it is the way my life was growing up. You see, I am from a family that was very physical with each other. What I mean by that, is there were no hugs and kisses, but fists and kicking. When I was a child, my parents fought like there was no tomorrow. If the food wasn't on the table by the time my father would get home from work, my mother would get a beating of her life. Sometimes he would burn her with the pan that she had used for frying the food that she had just cooked the food in. Sometimes he would pull her by her hair, and drag her from the kitchen. Don't let some food fall on the floor. That would be her dinner for the night. What I never understood, is why she would take all this abuse from him, when she could have walked away. It's not as if she had no place to go. She had people who cared for her, and who used to beg her to stay with them, and to get away from my father. She would always refuse, and would sometimes get angry at the thought of them having the nerve to ask her to leave her husband. She would definitely go by the vows that were made when they got married when it said, "till death do us part" for that was what eventually happened.

I will never forget the day that my father started to beat my mother early one morning. The screams were so unbearable for me, that I ran towards their bedroom and rushed inside to try my best to help her. What I didn't know was that I was running into a situation that will be forever etched in my mind. My father had my mother on the floor beating her to a pulp. Blood was running from my mother's mouth, as my father had her head in his hands, hitting it again and again on the floor. I couldn't let my father hurt my mother anymore, so I ran to the kitchen, and picked up the biggest knife I could find. I then ran back into the bedroom, and started to stab my father. I was only seven years old at the time so I could only reach but so far, but I did stab him in the leg several times. I did enough damage for him to stop beating on my mother. What I didn't know, was that my mother ended up turning on me for hurting my father. That was a big blow to me. I was totally confused. What was I to do? I tried to help my mother, and she then turns on me. Who do I turn to now that I'm in trouble? When I say I was in trouble, I really mean it.

The stab wounds from what I did to my father, had punctured a main artery in my father's leg, and he later died. When I heard the news, I couldn't believe my ears. I had actually killed someone. I actually killed my own father, trying to protect my mother. From that day on, my mother really went berserk. She would cry for days at a time, and wouldn't eat anything. She wouldn't even take a bath. All she did was keep calling out for my father. She hated to see me, and when she did, she would start to beat and kick on me for killing her husband. She told me that I should have stayed out of grown folks bedrooms in the first place. I was called stupid ass, a no good son of a bitch, you name it, I was called it. She even said that I should have been the one who died instead of my father. I was not the same person ever again after that day. Seeing my mother go into a world of her own, and knowing that I was the cause of what had happened to my father, made me the most confused kid in the world. I had no one to turn to, that I felt could understand me, and what I was going through.

The day of the funeral was surreal. My mother was uncontrollable. I had never seen her act the way she was acting. In fact, I had never seen her do a lot of things since my father died. She tried her best to pull my father out of the casket. To tell you the truth, she almost did take him out. It took four men to get a hold of her. It was hard, for she was kicking and screaming. After a while, she finally did settle down.

The Reverend Thomas, a short, stocky man with graying hair is wiping his face with a handkerchief, for he always sweats profusely. He begins the eulogy by saying, "Good morning everyone. We are all gathered here today for a homecoming, and to pay our respect to Mr. Martell Chancellor Harrington, Sr., whose life was cut short by no means any one's fault, but by being in a bad situation, at a bad time. Now, we have all been in situations where we had to call on the Lord to help us to get out of that situation. Can I get an Amen?"

"Amen Reverend"

"As you all know, we are here on borrowed time. Nothing or no one lasts forever. You all hear what I said?"

"Yes Reverend, tell them."

"Let me repeat myself, for I don't think that everyone heard me. Nothing or no one lasts forever. From the birds and the bees, to the flowers, and the trees, nothing lasts forever."

"Amen Reverend, Amen."

"From the womb, to the tomb is what makes a person who they are. What happens in between those times makes a difference. What I mean by that, is what one does in life is how one is remembered. Not to place judgment on anyone, but life is what you make it. There are times when you may feel that you want to take your own life when someone you love dies. What for? What purpose will it serve? Don't worry; you'll get your chance. Why rush it.

You have cut your life short; because you feel that you can't live without them. I have a news flash for you. You can go on. That's right. I know that it may feel that your heart is being torn out, but it will heal. God will make sure of that. He doesn't give you any more than you can bear. Amen. There are five stages of grief. "You hear what I said?"

"Yes Reverend, go ahead. Preach on" someone says in the back row.

"There are five important stages of grief. The first stage is bargaining. Bargaining often takes place just before your loved one dies. Pleading with God, or trying to make deals with God, by promising to stop a habit, or doing better in life, if that person would get a second chance to live. The second stage is Denial. Not believing that your loved one is gone. Not accepting the truth. We all go through this stage at one time or other. The third stage is Anger. Blaming the deceased loved one for leaving you so soon. In your mind, you can't believe that they would do that to you. The fourth stage is Depression. This is the stage where one feels hopeless. Feeling out of control, and numb. The fifth, and the very last stage is Acceptance. Accepting that your loved one has gone on to a better place. Even though they may not be here with you physically, they will always be around you spiritually. This is the time to get closer to God. This is why I am asking everyone to please pray for the family in their time of grief. Yes Lord, please give this family strength to keep on living. To the Harrington family, even though it may seem that you cannot live without this person that you truly love, you can. God knows this, and this is just a test of your love for Him. He doesn't want to see you in pain down here on earth. That is not His mission. He wants this to be a time of reflection. A time to remember all the things that you shared together, whether good or bad, for we are all sinners. No one is put on this earth a perfect human being. No one but Jesus Christ."

"Amen"

"I would like to say a few last words to the family. God loves you. Never hesitate to call on Him in your time of need. No matter what time, day or night. His phone is never busy. He is waiting for your call. May God bless each and every one of you."

I remember my mother just staring into space like a zombie. When the service was over, my mother walked out of the church with two nurses on each side of her, after trying to run back to the casket to see my father before it was closed for the last time. She had gone into her own world.

CHAPTER 4

(Temporary Custody)

It wasn't long before the social service agency came and placed me with my grandparents. They felt that I was in an environment that was not safe. I was even sent to a child psychologist to vent the feelings that had built up inside of me for my parents. The stay at my grandparent's house was very interesting. Every character that you can think of came through there. I ended up growing up pretty fast while living with them. I was taught the tricks of the trades of life. What interested me the most, was of how the women would dress up fancy, to attract the men that were coming to the house to have a good time. They would put on their best perfume, and their hair would be done real nice. They would walk around in their high heels, with tight clothes on, and get practically any man that would come along. They would take the men into one of the many rooms that my grandparents had. When they would come out of the room, it was totally different as when they had walked in. Their hair would be matted somewhat, and their clothes would be torn, or even worn backwards. The men however, were just as sharp as when they had first entered the building. What was going on inside those rooms that would make a woman do what she did over and over again? I would always ask myself. I surely couldn't ask my grandparents. I had to find out the secret on my own.

One night, while it seemed as though everyone was occupied, I crept up the stairs to follow behind a couple who were entering one of the rooms. I got on my knees, and was peeking through the key hole, as the man didn't waste any time in taking his clothes off, and the woman unzipped her dress, which fell to the floor. Then there was this odd thing that happened. It was as if they had done this before, or maybe the man was a repeat customer of the woman, but he took a leash and chained her to the bedpost. Then the man took a whip, and started to beat the woman with it. The man had on a black mask and a helmet, but what shocked me the most, was when he pulled out his penis, and started to ride the woman like a jockey in a horse race. Instead of a dog, this woman was pretending to be a horse. She was making sounds like a horse, which made me laugh, for this was something way out of my league. I couldn't contain myself with laughter. I'd never seen anything like this before. Not until I felt a large amount of pain come across my backside, that I knew that I was either dreaming, or I had the worst back pain a kid could ever have. I turned around to see that it wasn't a dream at all, and the back pain had come from the whack that my grandfather had given me for being on my knees peeping at grown folks doing what they do. He grabbed me by my shirt collar, and pulled me up from my knees. He lifted me up, and carried me to where my grandmother was.

"Look who I found peeking in a peep hole upstairs."

My grandmother turns around and says, "I wonder when you would start getting curious. I told you this little bastard was going to be a damn problem for us didn't I?

The only reason he's here, is because of the damn check I'm getting. Don't tell me that we have to lock him down in the basement," she says sternly.

"I think that we should teach his little ass a lesson that he won't forget. I bet you next time he won't go peeping anywhere else," says my grandfather.

"No, leave him alone for now. It's too soon," says my grandmother.

It was never too soon for me. After that day, my grandfather would come into my bedroom at night, and molested me while I was asleep. When I would wake up, he would cover my mouth, so that I couldn't make any noise. He would even threaten to kill me if I ever told anyone. One night, my grandmother walked in on us, and I thought that she was going to help me, but she didn't. She stood at the door and watched, as she smoked a cigarette. It was pretty clear to me that night, I had no one to depend on but myself. By the next morning, I had left and have never seen them again, until we were in court, and they were arrested not only for sexual molestation of a minor, but for prostitution, and illegal gambling. What a family.

I was then sent to another family, who treated me much better than my own flesh and blood, but no matter how much love that family showered me with, the emotional scars will always be there. At eighteen, I joined the United States Marines.

CHAPTER 5

(Loving)

It was a nice Saturday afternoon. The wind is blowing just enough to cool you off, without the sun getting a chance to beam down on you and burn your skin. Loving was feeling herself, for it was her twenty-first birthday, and nothing mattered to her. Her father had bought her a new car and it was sitting in the driveway with a ribbon around it. She called Gregory earlier to let him know that she would be over to the hair salon to get her regular treatment; hair, manicure, and pedicure. She didn't tell him about the car. She wanted to see his face when she arrived at the salon.

As she pulls up in front of the salon, one of the hairstylists whose name is Kyra says, "Damn, who is that driving that pretty ass baby blue Benz?" Some of the patrons get up to see who it is. One of the patrons says, "Whoever it is, they have a tight ass car." When Loving steps out of the car, Kyra says, "Oh, that's just that scrap Loving."

"Excuse me? Who in the hell are you calling a scrap? You had better watch yourself," says Gregory, taking up for his friend Loving. "You're just mad because nobody wants you that's all. She can't help it if she's all that."

"The Bitch thinks that the world revolves around her ass." Another one of the patrons then says, "Evidentally somebody else thinks so too. That car is spanking brand new. I love that color."

"You would love that color wouldn't you?"

"Damn right," says the patron. You may as well admit it. That car is nice."

"I wonder how many guys that she had to sleep with to get it. It had to be a hell of a lot," says Kyra.

"Stop hating Kyra," says the patron.

"Humph, I'm not hating. I wish she would stay the hell out of my husband's face. She just goes around picking up leftovers. Always trying to get somebody else man."

"Let me ask you something. Who had your man before you had him? I'm sure that you weren't the first cookie that he broke off. Now what do you have to say about that Scrap?" asks Gregory.

"At least I have a husband. She's still trying to find one."

"What does that have to do with anything? Shit, you're still insecure. Just because you're married, doesn't guarantee a monogamous relationship. Hell, I've been with so many married men who are on the down low, it doesn't make any damn sense. So don't stand there and tell me that your man is any different. He may not be on the down low, but he may be going down low with somebody else other than you."

"Alright now," says one of the patrons.

"No, I know my man. He would never cheat on me. I give him what he wants, how he wants, and wherever he wants it."

"Tell him baby girl," says another patron.

"You sound like a damn prostitute to me," says Gregory.

"That's right. I'm a lady with him on the street, and a freak with him between the sheets."

"Go ahead baby, tell him."

As they are all laughing and talking, Loving walks in, and everyone stops and looks at her.

"Good morning everyone," she says, as she thinks to herself how she can even turn a woman's head around when she walks into a room.

'Hey baby!" says Gregory, as he happily greets her with kisses on each cheek. "We were all here in a deep discussion about men, of whom as you know, is one of my favorite subjects. Come and sit down baby. You know that you're going to get the treatment today. Happy Birthday sweetie."

"Thank you sugar," says Loving. The young lady who had so much to talk about before Loving arrived says, "Hello Loving."

One of the other stylists says to the patron that she is doing hair on says, "Ain't that some shit? She is as fake as they come. You know why she's doing that? They are giving Loving a surprise party at that new club tonight. I guess she thinks that being nice to Loving is going to win her brownie points, so that she can slide her snake ass on in there. I wouldn't be surprised if she would show up anyway because that's the way she is."

"She's got some nerve if she does," says the patron.

"I love those sandals that you have on. You look so nice all the time," says Kyra.

"I Know. In fact, I look nice each and every day. Thank you though for the compliment," says Loving as she sits down to get a pedicure. The young lady rolls her eyes at Loving. Loving sees what the young lady does, and puts a smile on her face. She loves it when women do that to her. She knows that they want to be her friend, but feels that they aren't accustomed to the finer things in life, and she doesn't have the time to train anyone to be like her. Anyway, it would be impossible for any woman to try to live up to her expectations as a friend, unless she was born with a silver spoon in her mouth. They are the only ones of whom she feels can relate to her lifestyle. With the exception of Courtney, whose mother will do anything for her to keep up with Loving.

"My, aren't we quiet now. What happened, Kyra? The cat got your tongue?" asks Gregory.

"No, I'm finished with what I had to say."

"Okay then," says Gregory as he finishes up on his customer's hair. After getting a manicure and a pedicure, Loving gets her hair done by Gregory.

"I know that you're ready to let your hair down tonight. No pun intended," says Gregory.

"You know it," says Loving as she snaps her fingers, and moves her body. "You said that there was a new club opening up?" she asks.

"Yes, my friend Diego. He and a partner of his, are opening it up together," says Gregory.

"What's his friend's name?" asks Loving.

"His name is Chance, but I don't know too much about him though, but I'm sure you will find out."

"His name is Chance huh?" asks Loving.

"That's what they call him."

"He's not bad on the eyes either. In fact, he's soothing to the eyes if you know what I mean," says Gregory.

"Say no more. Once I get in to the club. I will take it from there okay?"

"Oh snap, my girl's gonna make some moves," says Gregory smiling.

"Don't I always get what I want?"

"Well, yes you do baby girl."

"That's if I want him. I have to check him out first, even though I do trust your judgment."

"That's settled then. Christopher and I will pick you up around nineish," says Gregory. When he finishes Loving's hair, he gives her a mirror to look at what he had done.

"You look beautiful," he says.

"I do don't I? Now tell me something else that I don't know." As Loving is looking in the mirror, she sees Kyra take her finger, and put it in her mouth as if she is gagging. She gives the mirror back to Gregory, gives him a double kiss on his cheeks, and walks over to the station where Kyra is standing rolling up a customer's hair.

"I saw what you did when you took and put your finger in your mouth. I know that you don't know any better. What puzzles me is that why would you gag on your finger, when your husband's penis is the same size?"

Kyra's eyes open wide and she tries to swing at Loving but misses. One of the other stylists grabs Kyra and holds he back, as she tries her best to get to Loving. She is swinging her arms, and is kicking at Loving.

"You Bitch. You're going to regret what you just said. My husband wouldn't be caught dead with you, you Scrap!"

"You may as well say that he's dead. Ding dong Mr. Limpy's dead," sings Loving, as she puts on her shades, throws her hair back, and switches out the door. When she gets out the door, she looks back and throws a kiss at Gregory who is shaking his head as he throws a kiss back at her.

"You know that you asked for that don't you Kyra?" asks Gregory as the stylist let her go.

CHAPTER 6

(They Meet)

Gregory and Christopher pick Loving up at her house around nine-thirty. Of course they didn't need to tell her how good she looks because she already knows that. When they arrive at the club, there are just a few people sitting at the bar. Gregory whispers to the bartender, tells Loving and Christopher that he will be right back, and goes towards the back of the club. As they wait for Gregory to come back, Loving asks Christopher, "It's pretty empty in here tonight isn't it?"

"It sure is. It's still a little early though. They'll be walking in here pretty soon," says Christopher.

"If not, I will be walking out of here pretty soon."

A short time later, Christopher sees Gregory coming from the back of the club and distracts Loving so that she doesn't know where he had just come from. Gregory nods his head to Christopher to let him know that everything is ready. Loving looks at her watch and wonders what is taking Gregory so long.

"Here comes Gregory now," says Christopher now relieved.

"I hope that I didn't take too long. I just had to look at everything in the club. Come on, let me take you on a tour. Diego doesn't mind. In fact, He wants to meet you anyway Loving," says Gregory.

"Same here," says Loving.

They start to walk towards the VIP section of the club when Gregory stops them and says, "Before we go any further, I want the both of you to close your eyes while I take both your hands and lead you to the room."

"This is so silly," says Loving.

"Just do it please," says Gregory, knowing that no one will have their eyes closed except for Loving.

"Now hold my hand, and you will change your mind about feeling silly when you see this. It's tight, I'm telling you."

When they enter the room, no lights are on. "You can open your eyes now," says Gregory. As soon as he says the word now, the lights come on. Everyone is surrounding Loving saying, "SURPRISE!" Loving holds her hands to her mouth, and her mother walks up to her and says, "Happy Birthday sweetie. I know that you thought no one remembered your birthday except for your Dad."

"You know I was upset don't you?"

"Yes, I do, but we had to keep it a secret from you, or it wouldn't have been a surprise, now would it?" asks her mother.

"No Mom, it wouldn't. Loving starts to cry, seeing so many people coming out to help her celebrate her birthday. They bring her over to a table where there is a large cake with many gifts and cards. "Oh my God! This is too much. I never thought that you all would do this for me. All I was thinking about was a gift. Thank you so much. Where's Aunt Maxine?"

"She's here. She'll be in here in a minute. You just relax and enjoy yourself. This is all for you. Maxine walks up to Loving and gives her a hug and a kiss, and wishes her a happy birthday. "You know that I wouldn't miss this for the world. Now, are you going to sit there and cry all night, or are you going to party?"

"You heard what your aunt said," says Courtney. As they are talking, Paige walks in with her sister Tara and says, "Happy Birthday Loving."

"Where's Autumn?" asks Loving.

"She couldn't make it, so she told me to tell you to enjoy yourself and she will talk to you soon." She then hands Loving an envelope.

"Thank-you. I'm glad that you both made it. There's plenty to eat and drink, so drink up" says Loving. Gregory, who is across the room talking to Christopher, comes over and introduces himself.

"Hello ladies. My name is Gregory, and I'm a very good friend of Loving."

"Oh, Courtney, you met Gregory at my Aunt Maxine's house on Thanksgiving. Gregory, this is Paige," says Loving.

"Nice to see you again Courtney and it's nice to see you again Paige. I met Paige at your Aunt's too. As you both should know by now, I'm gay, and that handsome man standing over there with the blue outfit on is my companion Christopher. I just wanted you to know this beforehand. Not that I think that you two may try to flirt with him or anything. But you are female, and he is a male, so there could be an attraction coming on. I just want to tell you from the start, that I am a very candid person, and in order for you to not get your feelings hurt, I advise you to not try anything okay? If that's understood we will get along just fine," says Gregory.

"It's okay with me," says Courtney.

"Yea, it's okay with me too," says Paige who is a little surprised by what Gregory said.

"Well then, since we've gotten that out of the way, let's party!" says Gregory as he throws his hands up in the air and snaps his fingers. He then walks over to Christopher, takes him by the hand and they go on the dance floor.

Paige stands there looking at Loving, and Loving says, "What you see is what you get from Gregory. He holds nothing back."

"I see. I came here to help you celebrate your birthday, and that's what we are going to do, celebrate," says Paige.

The music is pumping loud, and almost everyone is out on the dance floor. It had gotten to the point at one time that even the bartender is dancing as he is mixing the drinks. The music goes on for quite some time until the DJ turns it off, because Courtney went up to ask him to do it so that she could make an announcement.

"May I get everyone's attention please? As you all know, this party is for my good friend Loving Masterson. Loving come up here please." As Loving approaches the front, Courtney asks Gregory to come up to the front also. "Does everyone have a glass of champagne? If not, please get a glass. We would like to give Loving a toast. This is to you Loving. You have a heart of gold. I will be there for you no matter what, through thick and thin. We all love you baby," says Courtney.

Meanwhile, unbeknownst to them, Kyra has entered the building and is standing in the back by the door watching.

"I'm not going to make this a long drawn out speech, but I just want to say to Loving that to keep being the same person that you are, inside and out. Thank you for being you," says Gregory.

"This is getting to be a little too sentimental for me," says her aunt Maxine, as she starts to shed tears.

"Will everyone lift their glasses up so that we can take a drink for Loving? That is if you haven't drank it all yet. If you have, I would like for the servers to refill their glasses please. To a very classy lady. Here's to you Loving," says Gregory as everyone lifts their glasses and says, "TO LOVING," everyone shouts.

"We have a special surprise for you." The music begins to play softly, and then the crowd opens up. Loving hears someone humming a song that reminds her of her favorite singer. She hears the person start to hum just a little bit at first that catches her attention. The person seems to be getting closer and closer. He begins to sing, and when Loving finally sees who it is that is coming from out of the crowd, she almost faints. It is Vincent Lawrence. The balladeer of who is her favorite artist.

"I can't believe this!" says Loving, as she holds her hands to her mouth. "I just can't believe this!" She starts to flap her arms in excitement. Mr. Lawrence then says, "Believe it Loving, because I am here in the flesh to sing only to you, "Happy Birthday Baby." He starts to sing again, as tears roll down Loving's cheeks. All she can do is shake her head as Mr. Lawrence holds her hand while singing to her.

"What I wouldn't do to be in her shoes right now," says one of the guests. Kyra is now standing by the bar and says to herself, "Look at that fake ass bitch. I bet she knew all about this party, trying to play it off." After Mr. Lawrence finishes singing a song to Loving, he gives her a kiss on the cheek.

"This is one of the best parties that I've ever had. Knowing that I have my family and friends all here to help me celebrate my birthday, means so much to me. You just don't know how I'm feeling at this moment. This is wonderful. I want to thank everyone for coming, and to continue to enjoy yourselves." Mr. Lawrence sings a couple more songs, and then joins Diego at the table where he is sitting with several women.

"Why didn't you tell me that you knew Vincent Lawrence?" asks Loving.

"If I'd told you, it wouldn't have been a surprise, now would it? Anyway, my friend Diego helped me to set this up. In fact, let me introduce him to you now," says Gregory. They walk over to the table where Diego is sitting with Mr. Lawrence. Diego sees them coming towards his table, and gets up to greet them.

"Hello Ms. Masterson. It's so nice to finally meet you. I've heard so much about you from Gregory."

"Oh really," says Loving.

"Yes, there was nothing but nice things. You are more beautiful than I imagined. Have a seat."

"Thank you," says Loving, as she sits down.

"Diego is the one that helped me set everything up for you here. He is the owner of this club.

"I appreciate it that you let Gregory use the club for my party. It was very thoughtful of you."

"It was my pleasure," says Diego.

"Loving, you haven't met Mr. Lawrence formally yet. Vince, this is Ms. Taliyah Loving Masterson."

"What a beautiful name for a beautiful woman. I would ask you how you are doing, but to look at you, I see that you're doing just fine."

"Thank-you, I get that all the time." The other women at the table look at each other as Loving smiles at them knowing what they may be thinking of her.

"Loving, this is Mr. Vincent Lawrence."

While Gregory is introducing Loving to everyone, and they are talking, Chance is watching Loving from across the room. He doesn't approach her yet, but wants to wait until the right time. He sees that she is a very pompous person, and doesn't want to seem as if he is smitten with her, although he is just as smitten with her as every one else. He stays back and watches her, as she has a conversation with Diego and his friends.

After watching them for awhile, he finally decides to walk over towards them, and when Gregory sees him coming says, "Loving, there is someone else that I would like for you to meet. This is Mr. Martell Harrington."

"Hello," says Chance, as he stares into Loving's eyes. "My friends call me Chance. It's so nice to meet you." As he reaches his hand out to greet her, she feels a buckling in her knees. "Oh-My-God!" (she thinks to herself). "I don't think heaven can get any better than this, because the way I feel right now, it's as if I'm in heaven."

"Hello," she eventually mutters, as she is still staring into Chance' deep penetrating eyes, which are a light hazel color. Gregory notices the stares they both are giving each other and interrupts.

"Loving, Chance is a realtor, and is also a co-owner of this club with Diego."

"Oh really?" she asks, as if this is the first time that Gregory has told her. "As I told Diego earlier, this place is very nice. I want to thank you also for letting Gregory have my party on the opening night of the club. Thank you so much."

"Well, he is a friend of Diego's, so that was no problem," says Chance.

"I have to excuse myself now. It was nice meeting you all, and thanks again for your hospitality," says Loving, as she rushes to the ladies room to get herself together. She goes into one of the stalls, and when she comes out, and is at the sink washing her hands, a woman comes behind her, and warns her about Chance.

"Excuse me Miss," says the woman. You don't know me, but I've noticed that you and the man named Chance have been exchanging glances at each other throughout the evening. I'm here to warn you personally, to stay away from him, for he is nothing but trouble." The woman then takes off her shades and shows Loving her eyes. They are black and swollen. At first Loving is taken aback at the nerve of the woman of whom she doesn't even know, to approach her, until she sees the woman's face. She turns around and looks at the woman carefully and asks, "What do you want me to do about what some man has done to you? I don't know who you are, and really don't give a rat's ass. I don't even know if you really know who Chance is. Anyway, what you've been through is not my problem, so I suggest you had better take that pity party somewhere else, because this is a party for happy, attractive people. To look at you, there is nothing happy, or attractive about you."

Tears begin to roll down the woman's face, as Loving turns back around and looks into the mirror, touching up her hair and make-up. She sees the woman still standing there staring at her crying and asks, "How did someone like you get in here anyway? I don't socialize with people beneath me. I'm going to have to check and find out what's going on at the door. I know its opening night, but damn, it seems they are letting anybody in here. I can't have that, putting my reputation on the line."

"You are really dillusional aren't you? I'm here to try to protect you from a man who can eventually kill you." says the woman.

"And? Why are you still here? He hasn't killed you yet."

"That's because he doesn't know where I am. He can't find me." says the woman. Loving starts to laugh and says, "You mean to tell me, that you've come out from hiding from a man who supposedly could kill you if he finds you? To a club that he co-owns, risking your life just to warn me, (pointing to herself), a woman that you don't even know? I'll tell you who you should be hiding from. The people who are looking for you, to take you back to that institution, to put you back in that padded room. That's who you should be hiding from. Now, if you don't take your crazy ass out of here, I will have to get someone to escort you out."

"Please listen to me. I know what damage this man can do. Stay away from him, or you will regret it." As soon as the woman finishes saying that, Courtney walks in. The woman quickly walks out trying to hide her face as she bumps into Courtney.

"Damn!" yells Courtney. "I've seen people hurrying to get into the ladies room, but I've never seen anybody hurrying to get out."

"Who is at the door letting anybody off the streets in here?" asks Loving.

"I think it's the bouncers who work for Diego, why?" asks Courtney.

"Oh nothing, I just had a stranger approach me, that's all. It's nothing to worry about.

"If you say so," says Courtney.

"I need me a drink right about now," says Loving. They leave out of the ladies room headed for the table to get drinks. As they are walking across the room, Diego licks his lips, and says, "That friend of yours, Loving is fine."

"She's going to stay that way too," says Gregory.

"What do you mean by that?" Diego asks.

"I know how you are. You don't stay with one woman long. I don't want to see her get hurt," says Gregory.

"Oh, I'm not going to hurt her. I'll be gentle," he says now laughing with Vincent Lawrence, and Chance.

"Humph, since when have you been gentle? I thought you always liked it rough. That's who I always see you with, those rough looking women," says Gregory.

"Watch yourself" says Diego. "Why are you so protective of her? You don't even like women, so what's the problem?"

"Problem? I don't have a problem. I just don't want you to get involved with her, while you are still involved with many more that's all. Loving is like family to me. It is my duty to protect her from prowlers like you. She wouldn't give a thought about you anyway," says Gregory.

"Do I hear a hint of jealousy in your voice?" asks Diego.

"Hell no, don't even go there okay? That was in the past, and it was just a couple of times, so don't bring that subject up anymore. I must have been out of my damn mind anyway," says Gregory.

"You were out of your mind alright, and out of your clothes quick too," says Diego.

"If it was that good, I would still be coming back, now wouldn't I?" asks Gregory.

"What do you call this being jealous about your friend?" asks Diego.

"Please – I've gone on to something bigger and better, and I mean bigger, and with capital letters" says Gregory.

"Whatever you say. Just don't try to tell me what to do again. That's if you want to keep our little secret a secret."

"Hell, that's not a secret. Loving's family is just some of the people here, that don't know that's all. You see, everyone else knows who and what I am, and know that I am very proud to be who I am. I don't have to sneak around. I'm very comfortable with the skin I'm in sugar.

Its people like you, who try to be someone they aren't. Remember, I have nothing to lose by this, and everything to gain. So Diego, the next time that you think you have something to threaten me with, think again." Gregory then gets up from the table and walks away. Diego is speechless. All he can do is sit and watch Gregory as he walks away switching. He turns towards Vince, who is staring him in the face. He takes what is left of his drink and swallows it down real quick. Vince smiles and says, "Well, you know that Gregory has always been straight up about things. That's the only thing that he's straight about." They laugh about it. Even though Diego is laughing with Vince, he is not going to forget what Gregory said to him. They order another round of drinks.

CHAPTER 7

(Chance)

Chance is in his own world staring at Loving, and watching her every move. He is determined to get to know her. He feels that Diego doesn't have a chance with Loving. He could tell when she met him, how she paused and looked. He excuses himself from the table, and walks over to where Loving and Courtney are seated.

He first asks Courtney to dance just to throw off who he really wants, which is Loving. Courtney is so excited. She cannot believe that Chance is asking her to dance, instead of Loving, but she is not giving up dancing with him. As they are dancing, Chance notices that Courtney is coming on to him pretty strong. He thinks to himself that this could be the best thing that could happen, because he could get all the information he can from Courtney. Loving is distracted at first, from Chance and Courtney until Paige says, "I see that Courtney still doesn't know how to hold her drinks. Another whole side of her comes out. Even though they say when you're drunk, the truth does come out."

"Where is she anyway?" asks Loving.

"Well, I saw her earlier with some guy dancing, but I see that he is standing over there with Mr. Lawrence now. I don't know where she is," says Paige. Loving looks over to where Chance is standing, and he is staring at her. He gives her a wink, and a smile. She smiles to herself and says, "I guess Courtney doesn't know a good man when she sees one. I know I wouldn't have walked away from that."

"He is handsome isn't he?" asks Paige.

"Yes he is, and if he comes my way, I will not hesitate to latch on to him. I can't help it if Courtney is not used to fine men," says Loving.

"Oh, that wasn't nice Loving, but it's true," says Paige as she and Loving give each other high fives.

"All right now," says Paige.

"If a diamond shines in your face and you don't at least stop and take a look at it, what does that say about you?

That you don't know a fine gem when you see one, and there's only one chance to pick it up, for someone else is going to come right behind you and get it. You know what they say, "That diamonds are a girl's best friend," says Loving as she takes a sip of her drink. What they don't know is that Chance took Courtney home, for she was drunk and getting out of hand. He had searched her handbag, and found out the information he wanted about Loving. That is, her address and cell phone number. First, he took Courtney to her house and had sex with her, in which she was more than willing to do. She was no good to him after that, for he disdains women who throw themselves at him. What broke the camel's back was when she started calling him all kinds of names. That's what did it. He took Courtney by the arm, and twisted it, telling her to watch herself going around sleeping with a man that she doesn't even know. He tells her that he could kill her if he wanted to, but feels she was worthless anyway, so there wasn't a need to do so. That if she keeps up this habit of hers, someone else will do it. "Now, if I see you again, and I know I will, go the other direction. The next time I won't be so nice." He then lets her arm go, and leaves.

Meanwhile, back at the club, Loving and the girls are sitting around drinking, and notice that Courtney is nowhere to be found.

"I think that I had better give Courtney a call. She was a little tipsy the last time I saw her," says Loving.

"She sure was. I hope she's alright," says Paige.

"Courtney's a big girl. This is not the first time that she's done something like this. You know how she is when she drinks," says Loving as she waits for Courtney to answer.

"Hello," says Courtney, sounding as if she has just woke up.

"Courtney, where in the hell are you?" asks Loving as she turns on the speaker.

"I'm at home. I started to feel a little ill, so I figured that I had better leave."

"Oh, so it's like that?" asks Loving.

"She must have some man over there with her," says Paige.

"Why don't you mind your damn business? I'm not talking to you," says Courtney.

"I know how you are though, when you start drinking. You will take anybody home with you. You freak."

"Who are you calling a freak?" asks Courtney. Loving interrupts and says, "Okay ladies, this is not the Courtney and Paige Show. This is my party, and it's all about me, so please cut this short. Courtney, since you say that you aren't feeling well, I hope that the person that you're with, makes you feel better. You can go back and finish doing what you were doing before I called, and I'll talk to you later." Loving then clicks her cell to hang up.

"Whoever she's with must be good, for she left here without saying a thing to us."

"As long as we know that she's at home safe. Now where's my other drink?" asks Loving.

"Let this be the last one ladies" says Gregory as he walks to the table and brings a bottle of wine.

"Loving, this is for you from Chance. He wants you to know that even though he didn't get a chance to talk to you one on one, that he hopes that this isn't the last time that he sees you. Honey, if I were you, I would hop on that like a rabbit. He is a masterpiece. I can tell by the way his clothes fit his sculpted body, that he also has a master piece."

"You're crazy," laughs Loving.

"Well, it's the truth. I'm not going to lie to you. You had better hop on that. You can see these bitches anytime," says Gregory.

"Who are you calling a Bitch?" asks Paige. When she drinks, she wants to argue and fight someone.

"You answered. Now what does that tell you Bitch?" asks Gregory.

"I will take and whip your gay ass," says Paige trying to get up from the table. Tara pulls her back down, and Gregory says, "Pleeease, - no need to pull her back. She knows damn well she doesn't want any part of me. Now sit down, and try to act like a lady for a change, and stop making an ass of yourself," says Gregory. Paige doesn't say anything else after that. She sits back and rolls her eyes.

"As I was about to say before I was rudely interrupted, it is after two in the morning, and it's time to go home now. I'm so full of myself right now, that all I want to do is get in bed and curl up with my man. I suggest that you ladies do the same thing. If you don't have a man of your own, then borrow one. It's only for the night anyway, so what the hell. The next morning, you won't remember a damn thing. I used to do that before I met Christopher. I would go to a bar, a gay bar preferably, and meet a guy. We would go some place and get off, the next morning we'd go our separate ways. If the guy was married, I sure didn't care. It wasn't my ass that was on the line when they got home." He starts to look around for his friend Christopher. "Speaking of borrowing someone else's man, I just know that's not Christopher with two women wrapped around his arm, walking out the door. Now you know that I have to go. I'll see you later Loving," he says as he kisses her on both cheeks, and hugs the ladies before leaving. I will see you girls later. It's been real." He is ready to rush out the door, but comes back and reminds Loving about Chance.

"I won't forget." she says.

As Gregory walks out the door, he sees Christopher standing with the two ladies, and one is whispering something in his ear. "Excuse me Bitches, but you are holding onto the wrong man. I suggest that you get the hell away from him ASAP," says Gregory with an attitude.

The lady who had been whispering in Christopher's ear stops and looks at Gregory and laughs in his face. She then turns back around and faces Christopher again.

"I don't want to have to repeat myself," says Gregory.

"That's right, you don't. We heard you the first time. Who is this person anyway?" asks the woman.

"What?" asks Gregory. "What part don't your ass understand? Stay? The hell? or Away?" The woman then asks Christopher again who is Gregory. Christopher looks at her and says, "This is my partner, Gregory. The woman looks at him confused and asks, "You mean someone that you just hang out with right? Like a friend? Buddy?" asks the woman. Christopher looks into the woman's eyes and says, "No, it's more than that. We are lovers. Both women are standing in disbelief. "What the ....?" Come on, let's go." They rush down the street fussing with themselves.

"That's right. Keep on stepping. Find a man of your own!" shouts Gregory. Christopher watches Gregory as he yells at the women as they walk down the street. He is disappointed that Gregory pointed him out the way he did.

"That's enough!" he yells.

"What?" asks Gregory surprisingly?

"You heard what I said. That's enough. You have embarrassed me to no end," says Christopher.

"Embarrassed you?" asks Gregory (now getting upset). "Don't tell me that you liked those two bitches clamoring all over you like that."

"Well, they did act like ladies. Not the way you're acting right now," says Christopher.

"I can't believe what I'm hearing. Some bitches are all over my man, and I don't suppose to say anything. What kind of person would I be if I didn't?" asks Gregory.

"You didn't have to make an ass of yourself out here in front of everybody, and I wish you would stop calling them bitches, because they're not." says Christopher.

"What? Oh, hell no. You are not going to stand there and make me feel like I'm wrong for trying to take up for you," says Gregory (now trying to hold back tears).

"I didn't ask you to do a damn thing for me," says Christopher.

"You know what? You and those two BITCHES that you are taking up for, can kiss what I sit on. Which is very soft and smooth, and will be very appreciated by someone else, who appreciates someone as fine as me. Anyway, dumb ass, you are just as confused, because you told them that I was your lover. How are you going to go back and explain that?"

"I don't have to. They're bi-sexual too. I don't have to explain a thing to them. All I have to do is give them a call, and they'll come back." says Christopher. As Gregory and Christopher are arguing, and they have drawn a crowd, Chance comes behind Loving, takes her by the hand, and leads her away from the crowd.

"Where are you taking me?" she asks.

"You're coming home with me," he says.

"I don't go home with strangers," she says.

"I won't be a stranger for long. Not after tonight."

"You're very bold aren't you?" asks Loving.

"Just say that I go after what I want, and 99% of the time I get it," says Chance. .

"What about the 1%?" asks Loving.

"That's because I didn't want it," says Chance. "Now, stop asking so many questions and get in the car."

"O-o-h, I like a man who takes initiative," says Loving as she gets into the car. As they drive off, she sees that Gregory and Christopher still arguing.

"Poor Gregory, I hate to see my friend in a situation like that. I wish that I could help him."

"There's nothing you can do when lovers quarrel, but get hurt trying to protect them. Believe me, I know exactly what I'm talking about," says Chance.

"Sounds like you've been in a triangle like that before. Do I hear a sense of experience?"

"Yes you do, but I'm sure that we won't have that problem," says Chance.

"What makes you so sure?" asks Loving. Chance turns and looks at her, and says, "I take care of women like that. No woman ever argues with me out in the street like that. I won't allow it."

"How can you stop a woman from speaking her mind when she knows you have done something wrong?" asks Loving.

"I have my ways about doing things. I expect you not to try doing that."

"Well, I'm the kind of woman who gets what she wants, and if that's what it takes to get it, I'll do it."

"Listen to me. I'm saying this for your own protection.

"Don't ever try that okay?" Loving laughs and says, "Whatever." Chance looks at her, and thinks to himself that he may eventually have to teach this one a lesson, for she thinks that it's all a game. She seems to be very spoiled. I can tell by the way she was treated back at the club. What Loving wants, Loving gets. Except now, Loving has entered the world of Chance Harrington. That is a whole different thing all together. What she doesn't know is that I'm going to turn her life around 360. What she thinks she knows now about me, is very little. She's going to find out real soon, that things are not always what they appear to be. I'm going to take her for a ride that she has never been on before. Oh yes, I will wine and dine her for now, for that is what she's used to. Having men falling at her feet, giving her anything she wants, just to get with her. Talking to them, and treating them any way that she wants to. Some of the men never had been around a woman so beautiful, and they did what they thought would make her happy. No matter what the cost. All the while, she's taking it as a joke. We'll see how that turns out pretty soon.

They did have a whirlwind romance. As he said, Chance wined and dined Loving, and gave her everything that she ever wanted and more. Loving never had time for her friends anymore after that. It was all Chance. He was her world. They were practically inseparable. This went on for months and months until one day, they were coming home from a concert, and Loving, being the Diva that she is, says something out of the way to Chance. That was the worst thing that she could have done.

CHAPTER 8

(The 1st Hit)

"How did you like the concert baby? The seats we had were the best," says Chance.

"I've been to better concerts," she says, as she looks in the mirror primping her hair.

"What? You didn't like the concert or the seating?" asks Chance sounding disappointed.

"What difference does it make? If I said that I didn't like it, I didn't like it. No matter what it was," snaps Loving.

"What is your problem? I bring you out here, get the best seats in the house, and you still don't appreciate it."

"Whatever," says Loving as she shifts in her seat and looks in the mirror at herself a second time.

"You could sound more appreciative than that," says Chance glancing at her as he is driving.

"What do you want me to do? Jump up and down like a kid? Oh, okay, I know what you want to hear. Thank you so much Daddy. This was the best thing that anybody has ever done for me. I really enjoyed myself. Thank-you, thank-you!"

"I didn't say that you had to do all that. What's your problem?" he asks.

"I don't have a problem. You make it seem as if this was the concert of all concerts. It's not as if we went backstage to meet the performers or anything," says Loving.

"What's up with you? I try to take you to the best places, buy you the best things and you're still not satisfied."

"Maybe it's you that's not all that anymore," says Loving as she puts the mirror back in place. Chance has now lost his cool, in which he tried to keep. He takes his arm, and reaches over, grabs Loving's head, and slams it into the dashboard. Then he says, "So, I'm not all that now huh? We'll have to see about that won't we? Damn right I want you to jump. Not just for that, but for anything that I tell you to do bitch!" Loving didn't see this coming. She is so busy into herself that when her head hits the dashboard, she goes into shock. She couldn't believe what had just happened. Chance did it again and again, and then he let's Loving go.

Her head falls back on the seat as she blacks out. The next time that she wakes up, she is in bed with a terrible headache. Chance walks into the room and says, "Good morning sleepy head. I was wondering how long you were going to sleep." Loving sits up in bed and holds her forehead.

"I have the worst headache," she says.

"You don't remember do you?" asks Chance as he serves her breakfast.

"Remember what?" she asks.

"We almost had a terrible accident, and I had to stop and swerve the car real quick, to avoid the other car that was speeding."

"Why is my head thumping so badly?" she asks.

"Your head hit the dashboard, and I tried my best to hold on to you, but your head hit the dashboard anyway. You knocked yourself out."

"I did? You tried to save me?" she asks in a surprised way.

"Yes I did baby. You know I would do anything for you. I care a lot about you. Don't you know that by now?" asks Chance.

"Yes I do," says Loving as she gives Chance a hug. "I love you so much. Thank you for saving my life. I will never forget this."

"Don't worry about it. It's the least I can do for you. Now eat up your breakfast before your food gets cold. I know how you don't like cold food. You'll have me running back in the kitchen heating your food back up again. Look, I have to make some runs, but I'll be back a little later. You stay put and relax yourself for the day. Don't you worry about a thing." He gives Loving a kiss and then leaves.

Around a half hour later, Gregory calls to see what Loving has been up to lately since he hadn't talked to her in awhile. He starts to tell her about his friend Christopher.

"Loving, you aren't going to believe what I found out after all that mess that went down between Christopher and me. Honey, that bastard Diego told Christopher that we were lovers."

"We were lovers? You and I?" asks Loving. Gregory laughs and says, "No–o, not us. I'm talking about Diego and me. He told Christopher that we were lovers."

"Oh no he didn't," says Loving.

"Yes he did, and to top that off, he's the one that set Christopher up with them two bitches. You know that pissed me off don't you?"

"I know it did," says Loving.

"The reason why he did it was because I got after him because he wanted to get with you."

"Who doesn't? From the lady on the street, to the police walking the beat. Everybody wants some of Loving."

"Okay Diva, I heard that. Anyway, I approached Christopher and tried to explain to him that what happened between Diego and I, happened long before he and I met. He wouldn't even hear what I had to say."

"That doesn't sound like Christopher," says Loving.

"I know. He has changed so much. You know how much I care about him, but I'm not going to make a fool of myself either. I do have my pride. If he wants to be with those bitches, go ahead. I'm not going to run behind him.

"You know that you're lying to yourself don't you?"

"I know. I'm still so in love with that man it's ridiculous. He has a body that's so tight, and his dagger, is a mighty dagger. You know what I mean?" asks Gregory pondering on the thought of it.

"You know I do." says Loving

"Humph, Chance has one that has me crawling the walls for more."

"I can tell by the way he walks. He has a swagger about him. He has a dagger with a swagger," says Gregory laughing.

"He keeps me happy though. This morning, he brought me breakfast in bed."

"That was thoughtful of him," says Gregory.

"It was, wasn't it?" asks Loving.

"He does that all the time?" asks Gregory.

"No, he did it this morning because last night we went to a concert, and on the way back, we were almost in an accident. He had to swerve the car to avoid hitting the other car. I don't even remember, but I hit my head on the dashboard and blacked out."

"That's what he told you." asks Gregory, seeming suspicious.

"What do you mean, that's what he told me?" asks Loving defensively.

"Hold it now. I'm just making a statement. I don't mean any harm."

"You act as if you know something," says Loving.

"Since you brought it up, I do have some information that I think that should be passed on to you," says Gregory.

"What jealous ass person has said something now?" asks Loving

"I know that you don't want to hear anything about your man, but it is being rumored that he has a terrible temper. That if he doesn't get his way, he will strike."

"I can't believe that you even said that out of your mouth. I think that you're the one who's putting rumors out there. Who did you supposed to have gotten that information from?" asks Loving.

"A woman came up to me telling me to warn you about him. She said that his name may be Chance, but you are also taking a chance on being with him. That he's an abuser. He likes to beat women to make him feel more of a man." says Gregory.

"That's crazy, and who was this woman? You're going to tell me that you believe some woman that you don't even know? Be for real. I thought you were better than that. Don't call me telling me some crap like that. If you're going to be a friend, be a friend. Not a jealous friend who is upset because you aren't getting along with your lover."

"I'm sorry Ms. Diva. I've been worried about you, that's all. I didn't mean any harm. You know that I love you don't you?" asks Gregory.

"I don't know. For a minute there, I thought that you might have crossed that jealousy line with all the others," says Loving.

"I love my Loving. We go back too far to let anything or anyone separate us. We are forever friends."

"I love you too baby," says Loving.

"Aww, you're going to make me cry," says Gregory.

"What do you think I'm doing?" asks Loving.

"Let me stop before I mess up my mascara," says Gregory. Loving starts to laugh, and says, "That's right; we don't want to do that do we? Who's the Diva now?" asks Loving.

"I know. Let me stop. When are we going to get together? You know we haven't seen each other for some time. I want to see you sweetie. I miss this. You know I don't really care about those other bitches. They are okay, but they will never take your place," says Gregory.

"I know. I'm one of a kind aren't I?" asks Loving proudly.

"Yes you are, and that's the truth. I would like to know who has been doing your hair. What bitch has been taking my place with that? You know I'm the only one who can hook you up and make you look fabulous. Not to say you don't already."

"That's right, correct yourself Diva. Chance has this woman who comes here to do my hair."

"Comes over there to do your hair? Please. Let me stop before I say something, and we get into it all over again."

"Yes, you do that. This woman is okay, but she can't do my hair like you do it."

"Let me start doing it again then. What's the problem?"

"I tell you what. Let me come over there to see you and we can take it from there, on what needs to be done," says Gregory.

"Okay, we can do that," says Loving. She gives Gregory the address, and he tells her that he will be there later in the day. She gets up to take her plate into the kitchen, and almost falls down for she starts to feel dizzy. She puts the plate down on the dining table and then sits down in a chair. She waits a few minutes to get herself together and then gets back up. She walks into the kitchen, puts the garbage in the disposal, and puts the plate in the dishwasher. She then goes into the bathroom and when she sees herself in the mirror, she screams. She starts to feel on her face and her forehead, which has swelled to the utmost.

"Oh my God! My face!" She calls Gregory back and tells him to please get over there as soon as he can. He was there within an hour. When Loving opens the door, and Gregory sees her face, he is shocked. There are no words coming out of his mouth. He is so surprised.

"What happened?" he asks.

"This is the result of the accident that happened last night," says Loving.

"Loving, let me take you to the hospital," says Gregory.

"Don't you think that I should wait for Chance to come back?" she asks.

"We can have him meet us there. You have wasted time already. You should have gone when it first happened," says Gregory as he walks in and leads Loving by the arm. He takes her in the bedroom to put some clothes on. Right now, she only has a robe on.

"Wait a minute Diva. You need to wash your pooty-tang before you go anywhere. Go ahead, I can wait for that. You know you want that to smell fresh when you go to a hospital," says Gregory.

"What did you call it? My pooty-tang? You're crazy. I never heard anyone call it that before," says Loving.

"That's what I call it. You know that is the only thing that I'm jealous of about you," says Gregory.

"I don't know what you are ever going to say out of your mouth. I guess that's why we are so close. You keep me guessing, and always tell me the truth whether good or bad," says Loving. She goes into the shower and as she is in there, Gregory is getting something out for Loving to wear. Chance walks into the house. He calls out to Loving but she doesn't hear him because the water is running. He starts talking and tells Loving that he sees Gregory's car outside. As he walks in the room he says, "What's going on?"

"Oh, hello Chance, it's Loving. I'm about to take her to the hospital. She needs to see a doctor right now," says Gregory as he takes out an outfit from a closet for Loving to wear.

"No she doesn't," says Chance sternly.

"Yes she does. Either you're blind, or crazy as hell, so take your pick. Or do you want me to?" asks Gregory. "Did you look at her face this morning or was your head so far in her twot that you couldn't see a thing anyway?" Her forehead makes her look like a damn Martian."

"It's none of your damn business what she and I do in here. What the hell are you doing in our bedroom anyway? In our closet? You're the one with the problem.

I decide if and when she goes to the hospital or not. She is my responsibility," says Chance.

"Your responsibility? What do you mean she's your responsibility? She is not married to you. I'm taking her to the hospital whether you like it or not," says Gregory as he and Chance stare into each others face.

"What I like is for you to walk your ass out of here in one piece while you've got the chance," says Chance.

"I tell you what. Let me take Loving, my best friend of whom I've known for years, and of whom you've only known for let me see, not even a year yet to the hospital to get checked out, and there will be no problems," says Gregory.

"Who said that there was a problem?" asks Chance.

"There will be one if you try to stop me from taking Loving to see a doctor," says Gregory.

"You've got too much damn mouth for me," says Chance.

"I have too much of something else too. Don't get it twisted now. Even though I may act like a woman and have feminine ways, I'm still a man. I can take you down hard," says Gregory.

"Oh yea?" asks Chance.

"That's right" says Gregory. The last time a so-called man put his hands on me, he lived to regret it. Let me tell you what I did to him. I caught him with another person, and when I confronted him about it, he pushed me down on the ground, and then if that wasn't enough, he had the nerve to spit on me. Can you believe that? The bastard had to nerve to spit on me. That is one of the nastiest things that you can do to someone. Anyway, when he did that, he took the person that he was with, by the arm and walked away. He actually turned his back on me. I didn't take that lightly, and took out my blade. As I got up from the ground, I rushed behind him and sliced both his cheeks. That's right. I sliced both his cheeks, and walked away. I'm not talking about the ones on his face either. He didn't even know what hit him at first, because he was still walking with this person until people started screaming at the sight of his ass bleeding. So Chance, if you want to take the chance to try your best to hurt me in some way, think again. I am not the one," says Gregory.

While the two are arguing, Loving begins to hold her head and says, "Please stop arguing. I can't take all this. Gregory, will you please leave? I'll be okay." Gregory turns to her and says, "I'm sorry Loving, but you need to see a doctor, and since I am in someone else's house, and you do want me to leave, I will. There is nothing I can do." He then gives her a kiss on the cheek and says, "Make sure that you give me a call as soon as you can. Love you baby."

"Love you too. I will let you know." Gregory then walks out of the house not even looking at Chance who is standing at the door watching Gregory as he leaves.

"I'm going to take you to the hospital," says Chance as he helps Loving with her clothes and then they leave for the hospital. When they arrive at the hospital, Gregory is waiting there already. He doesn't say anything, and doesn't let Loving and Chance see him. He is making sure that Chance did take Loving to the hospital.

"Humph, I guess he does have a heart after all." When Loving was called to the back by the nurse, Chance goes in the back with her, but not before seeing Gregory walk in the front door. He approaches Gregory and says, "You didn't have to follow us here you know. What? You thought I wasn't going to bring her here? What kind of man do you think I am?"

"Do you really want me to answer that?" asks Gregory. Chance smiles at him and walks away. Gregory leaves, and when he gets to his car, he calls Courtney and tells her about the incident. Courtney tells him how she doesn't trust Chance, and she thinks that maybe it may not have been an accident. "I have this strange feeling about him," she says.

"You're not the only one. Apparently this man has a history of hurting women," says Gregory.

"What?" asks Courtney.

"Yes, when I first heard somebody say something like that about him, I thought that maybe they may have been jealous of Loving because when you see them together, they look like a perfect couple," says Gregory.

"What can we do to help her? If we say too much, she will turn against us and not talk to us at all," says Courtney. .

"Tell me about it. I had an argument about that with her this morning. She was about to cut me off then."

"I can't believe she was going to do that to you of all people," says Courtney.

"Well, she was about to. I had to bite my tongue. You know it doesn't take much for me to sound off," says Gregory.

"Don't I know that. I had better call her aunt Maxine and her brother Morgan to tell them about her.

"Let me call her brother Morgan!" says Gregory excitedly.

"This is not the time Gregory," says Courtney.

"I know, but it was worth a try. My day will come."

"I'm sure it will, but right now, we're wasting time. I have to call him so that he can get up there."

"We aren't being too paranoid are we?" asks Gregory.

"I don't think so. It's better to be safe than sorry. I will call him and at least let him know what's going on. I'll call you as soon as I talk to him.

"Okay, and I will let you know if I hear anything," says Gregory. He then goes home, for he feels that there is nothing else that he can do. He is satisfied knowing that at least Loving is at the hospital being taken care of. He is more at ease now.

CHAPTER 9

(The Hospital)

Gregory decides to call Christopher to see if they can patch up some things between them. When there is no answer, he leaves a message telling Christopher how much he misses him, and apologizes for what he had said and the way he acted.

Meanwhile, Courtney tries to get in touch with Morgan, but all she gets is his answering service. She decides to go up to the hospital herself to see what is really going on since she was close by. When she arrives at the hospital, she goes to the emergency room, and approaches the information desk to ask the woman about Loving. As she is standing at the desk, out walks Chance. She is a little startled at first because the last time that she saw him, he told her to stay away from him.

"What are you doing here?" he asks.

"I came here to check up on Loving. She is my friend you know?"

"You didn't seem like a friend when you spread your legs open for me the night of her birthday party," says Chance.

"I was drunk then, and anyway that was a big mistake. I would never do that again," says Courtney. Chance laughs at her and says, "You would never do that again huh?" he asks. "If I would take you in one of them back rooms, you would do it again if you had the chance and you know it."

"Yeah right," says Courtney.

"Yeah right," says Chance as he grabs her by the hand and leads her to one of the custodial rooms. Before he can close the door good, Courtney is pulling at his clothes. She kisses his chest and goes down on him, giving him oral sex. When Chance finishes releasing himself inside of her mouth, he pushes Courtney away, and tells her to get out of his face. She wipes her mouth, straightens her clothes, opens the door, and rushes out of the hospital. When she gets into her car, she begins to cry. She can't believe that she has done it again. What is it about this man that she seems to be so attracted to, that she can't get enough of him? She asks herself this over and over again. She is supposed to be Loving's best friend, and here she is wishing that she was Loving. Wishing that she could have what Loving has, even going so far as to have sex with Loving's man. She tries to make herself feel better by saying over and over again that Chance really loves her and not Loving. That Loving is not married to Chance, so she shouldn't have to feel so bad about what she's doing with him. As she sits in her car, out walks Loving and Chance. Loving has a patch on her forehead, and Chance has her by the arm. Loving looks up and sees Courtney sitting in her car and tells Chance that she wants to speak to Courtney for a moment. Courtney rolls her window down as Loving approaches the car.

"Hey girl," says Loving, happy to see Courtney. "As you can see, I'm okay. It looked worse than it was. There was no concussion or anything. Thank the Lord for that. I know that Gregory called you didn't he?"

"You know he did. So you're okay?" asks Courtney now distracted that Chance is standing right beside Loving.

"Yes I am, thanks to my man here," she says smiling at Chance.

"Hello Chance," she says as if this is the first time that she has seen him today.

"Hey Courtney, how are you feeling?" he asks sarcastically. Courtney keeps a poker face and says, "I'm feeling just fine thanks."

"That's good. I'm sorry that we can't talk any further, I have to get my lady home so that she can rest," says Chance.

"I understand," she says.

"I will call you tomorrow Courtney, because the doctor gave me some pills to make me sleep. Thank you for coming to check up on me," says Loving.

"You know that it was no problem," says Courtney.

"Yea, thanks Courtney. Be careful going home," says Chance.

"I will, and you young lady, just rest and take care of yourself," says Courtney.

"Now you are what I call a real friend. You came out of your way to come here to see if I was okay. I won't forget that," says Loving.

"You know I had to check on my girl. I couldn't let anything happen to you," says Courtney.

"You can keep thanking her another time. It's time for us to go home now," says Chance.

"Okay, bye Courtney," says Loving as she waves as Chance leads her to his car. He takes another look back at Courtney as she is sitting in her car watching them.

As Courtney is driving home, she starts to think about what she had done with Chance. "Oh God, I think that I'm falling in love with him. Loving is my friend, and here I am feeling weak in the knees every time I see her man. A man who had picked me first to dance with him, so why should I feel guilty about what I did or what I'm doing? If he really wanted her, he would have picked her the first time. I think the only reason he chose her is because it was her birthday, and all the attention was on her. Loving this, and Loving that. It's always about Loving. I always get seconds. I'm tired of that. I want and deserve just as much as she has, and dammit I'm going to get it, no matter what it takes. As she is talking to herself, her phone rings, and it is Morgan, Loving's brother. He wants to know if she is going to come over to his Aunt Maxine's house. Neither she nor Loving have been around lately, and his aunt wonders what is going on. Courtney tells Morgan that there is nothing wrong, and that she will be happy to come over to his aunt's house. She asks Morgan when does his aunt want her to come, and he tells her the weekend. Courtney then asks Morgan had he gotten in touch with Loving, and he said that Loving will be there. Courtney smiles to herself for she thinks that if Loving comes, then it means that Chance will be there too.

"Loving told me about the accident she had. I'm glad that you and Chance were there for her. I appreciate that," says Morgan.

"No problem. You know that Loving is my girl and I have to look out for her," says Courtney.

"I know you will. Well, I'll see you at my Aunt Maxine's over the weekend then," says Morgan as he hangs up the phone.

CHAPTER 10

(Family Time)

Meanwhile, at Loving's house, her mother Brooke is sitting in the living room having a drink with her husband, Maxine, and Elaine with their husbands, their mother Josephine, and another couple. They all are sitting around talking and laughing about old times, and the trouble that they used to get into when they were younger.

"Remember when your grandmother caught us peeking in Ms. Caroline's window?" asks David, Maxine's husband. They all laugh and nod.

"Yea, she crept behind us, and all of a sudden, I felt a pain come across my ass. I turned around and it was your grandmother. I mean we were down in that window too. We had our ass sticking out peeking down there. For Ms. Caroline lived in the basement apartment," says Levy.

"I will never forget that day, because we saw when your grandmother left to go out. We thought that maybe she would be gone for a long time. Ms. Caroline always kept her blinds open halfway, so we thought that it was a good opportunity to see what a grown woman looked like with her clothes off," says David.

"What we didn't know was, that your grandmother came back home sooner than we thought. It wasn't enough that she whipped our ass, but she took us home and our father beat us again," laughs Levy.

"My Nanna was something else that's for sure," says Maxine.

"She sure was. I remember when she took this big stick and beat the shit out of a man who she said had tried to hit her with his car, after he had pushed her out of it. Don't ask me where she found that big stick, but she had it, and tore that man's car up with him inside of it. You would have thought that a tornado had hit that car when she finished with it. The thing is, the man was still inside the damn car," says David.

"How in the hell did she do that? I don't know," says Levy.

"She was a stuntwoman even back then," laughs David. As they are laughing and talking, there is a knock at the door. It is their grandmother and Loving's great-grandmother.

"Hey Mom," they say in unison as each one of them give her a hug and kiss and the guys shake her husband Harold's hand.

"We were just talking about you," says David.

"Oh really," she says sarcastically as she tiptoes over to the sofa and begins to pull off her shoes.

"Thank-you Jesus!" she says, as she plops down on the sofa.

"What's wrong Nanna?" asks Elaine.

"These shoes were hurting me so bad in church today that they had me crying.

"No you weren't Nanna," says Maxine.

"Humph, my feet were hurting so bad, that I could hardly move them. To top it off, the Reverend had me to come up to the front, because he wanted me to do a solo. Honey, I thought that I would die. You know me; I was still strutting up to the front anyway. When I did get to the front, it seemed as if the pain in my feet hit me all of a sudden, and it hurt so bad that I couldn't even move. I started singing, and you know how church people are when they hear a song that they like. They are going to get up even before you really start singing good, and you know that I can sing. (Now we know where Loving gets her arrogance from). Well anyway, I tried my best to play it off as long as I could. The pain hit me again. It felt as if my shoes were squeezing my feet as tight as they could. I kept on singing, but then I started to cry. That really got to the crowd. Here they are thinking that I'm crying because of the song, but I was crying because my damn feet were hurting so bad. Now get this, I started scatting. Do you hear what I said? I started scatting to a church song. That was how bad I felt. I had gone into a zone that I couldn't get out of. When I did finish singing, I had to stand in the same spot for a minute because I couldn't move. To top that off, the music kept playing and the church members were still standing up clapping and shouting."

"What did you do?" asks Elaine.

"I tried to play it off by strutting back and forth, slowly of course, and then I strutted myself right out the door.

The church members loved it. They thought it was all a part of the act. When Harold and I were outside, I told Harold to hurry and get that damn car door open for I could hardly move my feet anymore. He was taking his time walking out like the people were clapping for him,"

They are all falling out laughing now. It wasn't enough of what David and Levy had said about Maxine's grandmother, she comes in and makes a joke about herself. It turned out to be a very nice time for them enjoying each other's company. Their grandmother did get her feet soaked and had them massaged by her husband, and after a few drinks she was feeling very good.

CHAPTER 11

(Tunnel Vision)

Loving is at the point now that all she sees and wants to see is Chance. He is her world and whatever he says goes. There isn't anything that anyone can say that can change her mind. She doesn't have the time for any of her friends for Chance is her first priority. It has gotten to the point that Chance lets women come to his house while Loving is there. He tells her that he has a very large family and that the women are his cousins. As always she happily greets the women thinking that they are related to him. She feels that she is being a part of the family and that by meeting his relatives she is getting closer to marrying him.

There have been times when the women would spend the night. A majority of the time she would leave them alone thinking that they needed some time to themselves to get acquainted again and would leave the house. One woman stayed at the house for two weeks. Chance told Loving that the woman was having problems with the husband who had been abusing her, so he let her stay until things cooled down between them. The thing is, even though Chance tells Loving that the women are his cousins, he is telling the women that Loving is his half-sister. Neither one of them have any idea who the other one really is. That's the way Chance works. Each one of the women thinks that they are the only one. That is until one of them catches on to what is really happening, and then they get to see another side of Chance; the dark

side. For example, the woman who tried to warn Loving
in the ladies room at her birthday party. She was asking
too many questions, for she felt that something wasn't
right. That Chance had too many so-called cousins that
were women, and why were they prancing around the
house in front of him with all but nothing on? She
wanted to know, so she did some investigating and
started to snoop around. One day, she approached one
of the women and started a conversation with her about
the woman's relationship with Chance. Come to find out,
the woman wasn't any relation at all to Chance, and that
she and Chance had been lovers for months. When the
woman confronted Chance, and he beat her so bad, that
she was afraid to even come out of her house because
she thought that Chance would see her and beat her
again. Eventually she moved away so that he couldn't
find her.

Loving is at that stage now where she feels as long
as Chance gives her all the attention she needs, there is
no problem. She has gotten to be friends with the women
who come over to the house to see Chance, and
sometimes they go shopping together. Not having any
idea that they are sleeping with the same man. How do
they do that you ask? Well, Chance tells each one of the
woman when he first meets them that what they have is
unique. That no one else could possibly have the
closeness and the bond that they each share together.
He tells the woman that no matter what she hears or
sees, to not be alarmed by it, because nothing or no one
can tear apart what they share. If asked about their
relationship at any time, to either ignore the question, or
tell them that it's personal. The last thing that he tells
her, which is the most important, is that if the woman
does tell someone, no matter how she starts to feels
about him, and he knows that she will eventually fall in
love with him, that he will have to not only cut off their
relationship, but also something off of her body. The
woman usually laughs if off thinking that Chance is

joking with them because he laughs along with them. Not knowing that he is serious about the whole thing.

Well, Loving got herself caught in that position this time. One night, she had just come home from her mother's house, and this time, she didn't park where she usually did, because there was another car in the spot where she usually parks when she stays at Chance. She doesn't see Chance' car, and thinks that maybe it is in the garage. She uses the spare key that she has to get into the house. When she enters the house, it is very dark, which is pretty odd for Chance, because he usually has a light that comes on automatically by a timer when he's not home. She thinks nothing of it, and goes on to take off her coat to hang it in the closet, and then she takes her shoes off not even turning a light on herself. She has to use the bathroom real bad, so she rushes into it and starts to use it. As she is using the bathroom, all of a sudden, there is a loud bang that hits up against the bathroom door. She is startled, but can't really move, because she is having a bowel movement which keeps coming down. There is another bang against the bathroom again, and this time the door opens up. To her surprise, it is Chance and a woman all over each other kissing. Loving and the woman scream at the same time. It is the same woman that she had been shopping at the mall with a week earlier to get that same outfit that the woman had on. What the f---k?! What are you doing here bitch?" asks Chance surprisingly,

"What am I doing here?" asks Loving, looking as surprised as they are. She is still sitting on the toilet as Chance is talking to her. "First of all, can I have some privacy so I can finish what I am doing? Talking about being rude, this is crazy," she says.

"Come on baby, let's take this somewhere else," says the woman.

"Hell no, this is my house and I can stay where I damn well please," says Chance.

"At least she has a little sense, seeing that I am using the bathroom," says Loving.

"You know what? You've got too much damn mouth for me. You keep talking, and I'm going to put something in it for you," says Chance.

"Shiiit, how in the hell do you think you're going to do that?" asks Loving.

"What did you say?" asks Chance, who is really mad now that Loving has messed his plans up. He lunges towards Loving, but the woman tries to hold him back and tells him that it isn't worth it. Chance stops, and acts as if he isn't going to do anything. He tells the woman that he is okay, and to go into the bedroom, he will be there in a few minutes. He just wants to talk to Loving alone. The woman says okay, and leaves the bathroom. As soon as she leaves out the door, Chance locks the door and starts to jump on Loving. First, he hits her in the face, which knocks her off of the toilet. As Loving tries to get up, Chance grabs her by her hair, and begins to put her head into the toilet where she has just finished and has not flushed it yet.

"So you want to talk shit huh? Well you can eat it too Bitch!" Loving tries her best to get Chance hands from around her neck and head. He keeps pushing her head in and out of the toilet. It's as if he has gone into another world. The woman hears this, and starts to bang on the door calling Chance and telling him to let her in. He finally stops and lets Loving go. Loving is crying uncontrollably and is spitting and vomiting everywhere.

"Clean your stinky ass up and then get the hell out of my house," he says.

Chance opens up the door, and the woman sees Loving and heads for the door. She gets into her car and rushes off. Chance will never see her again.

CHAPTER 12

(Loving Seeks Refuge)

One day, Morgan comes past Loving's house and sees a woman that he never saw before come out of the house with a suitcase. He gets out of the car and says, "Hello, is Loving home?" The woman looks at him as if he is from another planet. She walks past him not saying a word.

"Excuse me Miss but I asked you a question," he says. The woman is now walking towards her car and is ready to open the door when Morgan grabs her by the arm and says, "Listen, I don't know who the hell you are, but you have just come out of my sister's house with a suitcase, and you're not going anywhere without giving me some answers."

"First of all, I suggest that you take your hands off of me," says the woman.

"I suggest that you tell me who the hell you are, or I'm going to do more than just touch your arm," says Morgan.

"Who are you?" she asks.

"I'm the lady who lives here brother. This is my sister Loving's house. Now either you tell me who you are, or I'll have you arrested for breaking and entering."

"Okay, slow down Loving's brother. My name is Kyra. Your sister and I have become good friends lately. She asked me to come and get some of her clothes for her. I saw you at her birthday party at the club."

"How come she didn't introduce me to you?" he asks. "I was introduced to all of her close friends."

"Well, Loving and I were not on good terms then. In fact, I crashed the party. You see, I wasn't invited, but I knew that it was going to be a nice one, and I knew everybody who was anybody was going to be there. I just couldn't be left out of something like that."

"How come I don't believe you?" asks Morgan still staring at her.

"That's not my problem. I know what your sister told me to do. If you have any questions, talk to her. If you were as protective of her as you seem to be, you would know what's going on in her life right now," says Kyra.

"What do you mean by that?" he asks.

"Well, I'm not one for gossiping, but it appears that your dear sister is being taken advantage of by her male friend."

"I should believe someone who has just come out of her house with a suitcase in her hand? Look sister."

"The name is Kyra."

"Look Kyra, I don't know what this is all about, but you aren't going anywhere until I find some answers. You possibly couldn't know Loving well, because she doesn't put up with crap from no one. A man too? Who would even think of trying to hurt her? Men fall at her feet. She never had problems with men at all," says Morgan.

"Don't I know it? I used to hate your sister with a passion for that. Even though I'm married, I still hated her for being so pretty. Not until I started noticing the marks and bruises on her body that I began to feel for her. Everything isn't always what they appear to be."

"How did you get to see her bruises?" asks Morgan.

"When she comes into the salon to get her hair and nails done, I started to notice then that something wasn't right. I couldn't approach her at first for we had words before so I didn't say anything. Not until I saw her the other day did I realize that I had to say something to her. Even though she is still pretty, that glow about her is slowly fading away. First, I talked to Gregory about it. I told him that I had been in a relationship that was horrible before I was married, and it seemed to me that Loving was going through the same stages that I had been through. I know that I could have been wrong about the whole thing, but I wasn't. She opened up to me and let me know that her friend had been hitting her, but he doesn't mean to do it. She feels that he loves her, and wants the best for her. She says that she knows that she can get out of hand sometimes, and he has to pull her back. That it's her fault when she gets him mad."

"Who is this so-called man?" asks Morgan, now mad at what Kyra is saying.

"His name is Chance."

"Why don't I still believe you?"

"Because it's your sister that I'm talking about, and you don't want to hear that she's being abused."

"What I don't understand is, why did she pick you to come over here to get some things for her? She has other friends.

"She doesn't want them to know that's why. Look, I tell you what. Come with me, and I'll take you to where she is. That's the only way you're going to believe me."

"Okay, I'll follow you in my car. Don't try any tricks," says Morgan.

"I don't play games when there is something as serious as this," says Kyra.

"I'm just warning you," says Morgan as he gets in his car, and begins to follow behind Kyra. Kyra feels that she may be betraying Loving by telling Morgan where she is hiding out, but feels it may be for the best. Why did I get involved in this shit?" she asks herself. "I have problems of my own to deal with, and here I am helping Loving out. Oh well, I had to do something. Seeing Loving like that, brings tears to my eyes. I hate that bastard for doing that to her."

As she pulls up to the driveway, she uses the remote to the garage to open it, and parks the car. Morgan is right behind her, but he parks on the street. He gets out of the car, and hurries into the garage where Kyra is waiting for him. When she enters the house and walks into the living room, Gregory, her husband Frank, and Loving are sitting around talking. When Loving sees Morgan walk in with Kyra, she jumps up, and is about to run out of the room. Gregory stops her, and she says, "You lied to me!" Why would you bring my brother here?" she shouts.

"I'm sorry Loving, but your brother saw me coming out of your house with a suitcase, and started questioning me. I had no other choice but to let him know what was going on," says Kyra.

Kyra introduces her husband Frank to Morgan. Frank tells Morgan that his sister Loving will be safe with them for he is a police officer and he is quite sure that Chance will not try anything while Loving is in his house. Morgan thanks Frank and Kyra for helping to protect his sister. He is surprised to see and hear all the things that Chance had done to Loving. He had no knowledge of the pain and suffering of his sister in the hands of a so-called man. The more they tell him, the more he wells up inside, wanting to kill Chance. He asks Loving why she didn't tell him about it, and Loving said that she was too ashamed. That she knew that it would kill their mother if she knew what was going on with her and Chance.

CHAPTER 13

(Courtney's Betrayal)

Courtney knows that Loving is not with Chance, so she feels that this is her opportunity to go over there as quick as she can, to see how far that she can get with him. "The Bitch doesn't know how to treat a man, that's what her problem is. I tell you what, since she doesn't know how to handle him, I sure will." She then goes out to the local mall and gets her hair and nails done the same as Loving does. She even has tracks put in her hair to make it as long as Loving's.

"If this is the kind of woman that Chance is attracted to, then this is what he will get," says Courtney as she walks out of the mall with a new hairdo and all.

When Courtney gets to Chance' door, she rings the doorbell. She turns her back towards the street, so that Chance can only see the back of her when he looks through the peep hole. When he looks out, he hurries to open the door thinking that Loving has come back. When she turns around, he finds out that it is only Courtney who has changed her appearance to look like Loving.

"What the...?"

"Don't say a word. All I want you to do is to look at what you've been missing. I know that you told me to leave you alone, but I figure if I can't beat em', join em'," says Courtney, as she walks pass Chance into the house. When she gets in there, she swirls around to let Chance see the transformation she did to herself to look like Loving. Chance is still standing at the door looking at her with wonder. When he finally does close the door, he asks her what the hell is she supposed to be doing by changing herself that way?

"Like I said before, "If I can't beat em', join em'. Which means since you like women who look like Loving, I may as well look like Loving too," says Courtney. Chance thinks to himself that this woman is actually crazy to think that if she would only change her appearance to look like Loving, that I would actually want her. He now knows that she wants to take Loving's place, and he is going to treat her just as worse as he does Loving. For a woman to pretend that she is Loving's best friend, and the first chance she gets, she gives up her body to the man of that best friend, is no woman at all in his eyes. She is being treated as a whore and nothing else.

"Have you ever heard the saying, "The grass always looks greener on the other side?" he asks.

"Yes I have, and I have been on both sides. I've seen the way Loving lives, and I've seen the way you and Loving are together. Now what's the problem?"

"Nothing at all. So you feel comfortable coming over hear trying to seduce me, while your best friend isn't here?"

"Definitely. I know what's going on, for she tells me everything. I know where she is, and who she's with. Of course I know that you don't know, but you will soon enough. All I want from you is to take care of my needs, and everything will be fine. I'll be happy to tell you everything that your precious ears want to hear and can take."

"You are definitely one of a kind, I tell you that," says Chance.

"I'll take that as a compliment," says Courtney, as she walks closer to Chance, and gives him a kiss. She starts to grab on his clothes, and he says, "Wait a minute, hold up baby. This is not a race now. We've got time. Why rush something like this. We both want something from each other right?"

"Um hum," moans Courtney, as she starts to kiss on Chance again. He decides to put up with it, until he gets all the information he needs from her, and then he will throw her away like trash, for that is what she is, nothing but trash to use and throw away. He leads her into the bedroom and when he touches her body, he realizes that she came over to the house prepared for she had nothing on under her coat.

"Whoa!" says Chance surprised. You really did come prepared didn't you?"

"Why waste time taking off my clothes when there is nothing to take off? You see, I am just like Loving," she says smiling.

Chance looks at her with nothing but distaste. She falls on the bed backwards, but Chance turns her over and begins to penetrate her anus without any lubrication. He knows that it will hurt her more, and that is what his mission is to do. Courtney tries to stop him, but he gets rough and pulls her hair as he is doing it.

"What are you doing?" she asks.

"Sh-h-h, this is how you like it don't you?" asks Chance.

"No-o, not this rough," says Courtney.

"This is the way Loving likes it, and don't you want to experience what Loving experienced? Now, just relax and enjoy the ride," says Chance, as he rams his penis into her harder and harder.

"It hurts too bad!" shouts Courtney. Chance ignores her cries, and is in his own world now, as he is steady pounding into Courtney's anus. To Courtney, it seems forever, but she thinks that she had better be quiet and take the pain, because Chance may not want to see her again. "If Loving can take him doing this to her, I know that I can," she thinks to herself.

When Chance is finished, he turns her around and makes her have oral sex with him after just taking his penis out of her anus. Courtney gags at first but goes through with it. She has fallen in love with him and will do anything he wants to make him happy. When Chance finishes releasing himself in her mouth, he walks to the bathroom and takes a shower leaving her sitting on the side of the bed. Courtney wipes her mouth and starts to go into the bathroom with Chance to take a shower. When Chance sees Courtney ready to get into the shower with him, at first he hesitates. He then realizes that he didn't get the information that he needs from her yet. He sweet talks her as he washes her body. Courtney is in heaven now thinking that Chance really does love her. It's just that he has his own odd way of showing it. What she doesn't know is that Chance doesn't give a damn about her. She is somebody who he can get what he wants out of and then throws away.

When they get out of the shower, Courtney starts to talk on her own about Loving before he gets a chance to mention it.

"You know that Loving is going around saying things about you. That you two are going to get married, and how you cater to her, and give her everything she wants. What I don't understand is, if she is getting all that from you, you wouldn't be all over me like this. Then again, I can give you what you like. She is so into herself, how can she give anything to anyone else?" she asks, so proud that she has satisfied Chance sexually.

Chance looks at her as he is drying off, and thinks to himself how dumb this bitch can be. She really thinks that I'm into her like that. Look at her. I do give Loving some credit, but this broad actually thinks that she can take her place. He then laughs to himself.

"What's so funny?" she asks.

"You," he says.

"Me? What did I say that was so funny?" she asks.

"Nothing in particular, I just like to hear you go on and on about Loving that's all."

"Oh you do huh? I have a news flash for you that I bet you didn't know. I hope that you don't take this lightly."

"Spill it," says Chance.

"I found out that your sweetheart Loving has been stepping out with Kyra's husband."

"What do you mean stepping out?" he asks.

"Stepping out," she repeats. "They are seeing each other. Having sex behind Kyra's back, and yours too I may add."

"How did you find out, and who the hell is Kyra?" asks Chance surprisingly.

"Kyra is a lady who works at the salon that Loving goes to. I've been seeing him and Loving together a lot lately," says Courtney lying.

"That doesn't mean anything. I can't go by that. They could just be friends," says Chance.

"I could be a millionaire too," says Courtney smiling, for she knows she is about to stir up some trouble.

"I know that Loving wouldn't do that to me," says Chance.

"Okay, but I know what I know. Kyra and Loving do not like each other at all. They are always arguing when they see each other.

Chance plays dumb by asking a lot of questions. Courtney is so happy to get all of Chance attention, that she starts to tell everything, even where Loving is.

CHAPTER 14

(A Surprise For Chance)

Courtney has been feeling nauseated, and can't seem to keep anything on her stomach lately. At first she thinks that maybe it is the flu that is going around, until she starts to think about when she had her last period.

After washing up and toweling off, she opens the pregnancy test that she had purchased the day before, to see if it comes out positive or negative. She is praying that it comes out positive, for she wants to have a baby by Chance so bad. It comes out positive. She looks surprised, and is jumping up and down in the bathroom, happy at the results. She lets out a small scream, and hurries to get her telephone to call Chance.

"Hello," he says groggily.

"Hello sleepyhead. How is my Prince Charming today?" she asks.

"I don't know about Prince Charming, but I'm doing just fine," says Chance.

"That's good to hear. In fact, I have some good news to share with you. Do you mind if I come over to share it with you? It's just that I want to see your face when I tell you. I am so excited that I can hardly contain myself!"

"Okay, if it's that important, I'll come over there," says Chance.

"Okay, I'll be right here waiting," says Courtney, as she clicks the phone, and starts to dance around the room. "I'm having his baby! I'm having his baby! Yes! Yes! Yes!"

She hurries to put on some clothes, and rushes over to the window to watch for Chance. He rings the doorbell, and as soon as she opens the door, and before he gets in the door good, she jumps into his arms.

"What is this all about?" he asks.

"Come sit down, for I want you to be comfortable when tell you the good news. I know that you are going to be as happy as I am about it."

"No, you come and lay down with me, and give me some of that happy ass booty of yours before I hear anything else. Then we can talk, and talk, and talk," he says, as he holds Courtney by her waist, and leads her into the bedroom.

After they are finished, Chance sits up in bed, and says, "Okay, okay, what is this all about? Tell me."

"Okay, here goes - I'm pregnant!" she shouts and claps her hands.

"You're joking aren't you? If not, you'd better be," says Chance.

"Why would you think that I'd be joking about something like this?" asks Courtney. (Thinking in her mind that Chance loves the idea of her being pregnant).

"Just as I said before, you had better be joking." Courtney is getting upset now, for she thinks that Chance should be jumping up and down like she was earlier to hear of her having his baby.

"Like I asked you before, why would I be joking about something as serious as this?" asks Courtney.

Chance gets up off of the bed and starts to put on his T-shirt, and shirt, and is not saying anything. He then puts on his socks and pants, then his shoes. Courtney is going on and on about how much she wants to have a child by Chance and it was just a matter of time before she would get pregnant anyway. That now was the best time. Chance, who has his back turned away from Courtney, turns around, and slaps her in the mouth. Courtney is startled, and holds her hands to her mouth. She lets out a scream.

"Shut the hell up! Let me talk now, and you listen. I don't know who the hell that you think you're dealing with, but you have crossed the wrong one this time. You told me that you were on the pill, and we even used condoms to make sure that this kind of thing wouldn't happen. Now, you're standing here telling me that you are pregnant? Don't play with my intelligence okay?" Now what other guys were you having sex with that you're trying to put this baby on me? Don't even try to say out your mouth that there was no one else, because I know that's a lie. As hot as your ass is, I know there's a slew of them that could be the father. I know how much of a slut you can be."

"What? There's not anyone else. You're the only one that I've been with, and yes I was taking the pill, until I fell in love with you, and wanted to have a part of you in my life forever," says Courtney.

"The only part of me that you're going to see, is the back of my ass when I walk out the door, and never come back," says Chance.

"I don't think that you should do that if you knew what I knew about you," states Courtney. Chance stops in his tracks and asks, "What are you talking about?"

"I did a background check on you, and I know all about you, Mr. Martell Chancellor Harrington. Yes, I think that you should sit yourself right back down or I will take this information and spread it to the world."

"I will tell Loving of how we have been having sex ever since the night of her birthday party, and how you crave for me every chance you get. You don't want Loving. What does she have that I don't have?

"You don't know a damn thing about me. If you did, you wouldn't try to do something stupid as this. Do you really think that I would have you over Loving? Be for real baby. I wouldn't be caught dead with you. Another thing, why be so desperate to go through all this, just to get pregnant by me?" asks Chance.

"I know that you have plenty of money. That's what's needed in this world to survive. You got it; I want it, and more. Courtney goes to her drawer, pulls out a folder, and waves it at him. "I have your life in my hands. Now, if you don't want to play by my rules, I will have to go to the Po-Po," laughs Courtney as she swerves around, smiling to herself. If anything happens to me, I have made copies of this, in case they don't hear from me for a certain amount of time. I told them to give the information to the police."

"The Po-Po? Ple-ease! It's going to take more than that to scare me. In fact, go ahead, do you need a ride? You stupid ass Bitch! Stay the hell away from me before I do something that I know I won't regret, because you deserve it. I think that you've been looking at too much damn television, if you think that's the way it goes.

"Okay, you faggy-ass Bitch! See what I do if you walk out that door, and deny our baby," says Courtney.

Why did she call him that? As soon as he hears the word faggy-ass, and then to top it off, with Bitch, he turns around and grabs Courtney by her neck, and swings her around the room. It happens so fast, that Courtney loses her balance and falls to the floor. When she tries to hurry and get up off of the floor, Chance starts to kick her, and he keeps kicking her while she tries her best to get up.

"What-the-hell-did-you–call-me-?" asks Chance as he steadily kicks Courtney. Courtney realizes that she is in danger, and tries to shield her face and body from the kicks, by going into a fetal position. It is too late for that. The damage was already being done, for Chance is steadily kicking her in the stomach too. He wanted to make sure that she would never have his baby. Courtney pleads for him to stop, but to no avail. Chance then walks over to pick up the folder that supposedly has the information about him, and tells Courtney that if she doesn't get rid of the baby, that the next time that he sees her, he will kill her and the baby, and to take that to the bank. He then opens the door, and slams it, not even looking back.

A few weeks later, when Courtney had finally gotten herself back together from the beating that Chance had given her, she starts to think of ways to find someone else to claim the baby that she is supposedly carrying. In fact, she is not pregnant at all. When she went to her doctor she was told that she wasn't. She told the doctor that he didn't know what the hell he was talking about, and that she was pregnant, and had been for several months. The doctor told her that she had miscarried. She realized it was from the trauma from the beating that she had taken from Chance. Even though she had been bleeding a lot lately, she didn't think that it was from a miscarriage. The doctor suggested that she see a psychiatrist, and she and curses at him before leaving his office. She has her mind set on having a baby, but is afraid to tell Chance the truth, so she stays away from anywhere she thinks that he may be. She is determined to have someone take care of her, whether she has a baby or not. If it takes lying about being pregnant to get someone to take care of her, she will do it. She hates it that Loving doesn't have to do much to get anything that she wants. Then an idea comes to her head as she leaves the doctor's office. She thinks about Levy, Loving's uncle. She did have sex with him without a condom. Well, she had sex with a few men without a condom, but Levy also has quite a bit of money to take care of her for the rest of her life. All she has to do is threaten to tell his wife, and that should do it. She knows that she is supposed to be Loving's best friend, but hell, Loving gets everything that she wants without a problem at all. Why does she have to go through so much just to live comfortably? "I am so tired of living in Loving's shadow. I want what she has, and I'm going to get it too. A girl's got to do what a girl's got to do. Someone's going to have to pay for it," says Courtney to herself. She decides to wait for what she thinks is the right time, and then she will spring it on him. What can he do but pay her to keep her mouth shut right? Time will tell.

CHAPTER 15

(Courtney's Plan)

A few days later, Courtney calls Loving just to get a feel of what has been going on since the last time that she had seen her. Loving tells her that she misses her, and that to come over to her aunt Elaine's house, for that is where she will be so that they can catch up on things.

"What a coincidence," says Courtney. "It can't get any better than this. It must have meant for this to happen. How else could this be so easy?" she asks herself. "This is one time that I can say that I love to be around you Loving, for you have set the right time and place for me to make my move. Ms. Courtney is going to get her some cash. There's nothing or no one that can stop me now, that's for sure."

When Courtney drives up in front of the house, Loving and her aunt Maxine are standing outside and greet her as she gets out of the car. Loving comes over and gives Courtney a hug, and then Courtney hugs Maxine.

"How have you been baby?" asks Maxine to Courtney.

"I've been pretty good and you?" she asks.

"You know me, I'm fine, look, fine, and even when I'm not feeling well, I'm still fine," she says.

"I heard that," says Courtney.

"Not only do you hear it, but you had better believe it too," says Maxine, as she switches into the house. Loving and Courtney look at each other and Loving says, "Well, you know how I feel, the same way as she does." Then they both go into the house and Elaine says, "Hey Courtney, where have you been lately? We haven't been seeing you around. You know Loving talks about you all the time."

"Hello Ms. Elaine. I've been a little busy lately with my Mom. She feels that I've been neglecting her so I've been spending some time with her. You know how mothers can be sometimes."

"Don't I know it. Glad to see you again though. Go ahead and enjoy yourself with my niece. I know that you two have a lot of catching up to do."

"Thank you," says Courtney as she walks away. As she walks towards the living room, she sees Levy and David in the den talking and looking at a football game. Levy sees her at a glance, and takes a large gulp out of the bottle of beer that he is drinking. Loving calls her name, and she hurries to where Loving is sitting in the living room.

"Do you want anything to drink now before we eat? asks Loving.

"No, not right now," she says.

"You look a little different," says Loving to Courtney.

"She sure does," says Elaine, as she walks in as Loving is talking to Courtney.

"You two have been friends for so long that you have started to look almost like twins," says Maxine.

"I wouldn't take it that far," says Loving.

"That is a compliment," says Maxine.

"On who's part? Does she look more like me, or do I look more like her?" asks Loving.

"Courtney is looking more like you, of course Diva," says Maxine.

"That can't happen, because she may try to imitate me, but she can't duplicate me," says Loving.

"What did you do to yourself anyway?" asks Elaine.

"I know one thing that she did, was to buy her some more hair and then style it just like mine," says Loving.

"There's something else about her too. I can't put my finger on it yet," says Elaine.

"I'm still sitting here," says Courtney. "You all are talking about me as if I'm not here. If you want to know something, just ask."

"I'll take it as a compliment that you want to look like me. As long as you don't go after my man, you and I will be friends forever. I already know that you wouldn't do anything like that to me anyway, so I'm not even worried about that."

"Let me tell you something baby, and I want you to never forget this. Don't ever keep talking about, or keep bringing your man around other women. That's an invitation right there. No matter how close that you and that woman are supposed to be," says Maxine.

"I know that Courtney wouldn't do anything like that to me. She is like a sister that I never had. I tell her everything," says Loving.

"Have you heard of the phrase, "Loving eyes can't see?" asks Maxine.

"No, what do you mean by that?" asks Loving.

"Well, it's when a person, no matter if it's a man or woman, is so in love with another person that no matter what he or she does to them, that they can't see it in front of them what everyone else sees. Take for instance, Courtney here, who has been your friend for many years, decides to flirt with your man right in front of you. You don't even think anything about it, because you trust her. The thing is, Courtney and your friend are having an affair behind your back, and you have no idea that it is happening. That's one instance of that phrase," says Maxine, not knowing that what she has just said was so true. Courtney is now feeling a little uncomfortable, because she thinks that maybe Maxine may know something, for how else would she come up with a phrase like that?

"I never heard of it, but like I said before, that will never happen with Courtney and me. We are friends till the end. Isn't that right Courtney?"

"That's right Loving. I would never do anything to hurt you."

As they are talking, Morgan walks in and says, "Hey everybody, how are my favorite women doing? Before anyone can answer, he then says, "Something smells real good. What is that you're cooking?"

"A little bit of this, and a little bit of that," jokes Elaine, as Morgan walks over and gives her a kiss on the cheek.

"I would like to have some of a little of this, and a little of that then," he says.

Courtney sees Levy coming out of the den and excuses herself to go to the bathroom. She casually walks past him and whispers, "I'm pregnant." His eyes widen and Loving sees him, and asks, "What's wrong uncle Levy? You look as if you've seen a ghost. I know that I haven't been gone that long."

"He tries to straighten up and clears his throat. Oh nothing's wrong. It feels like something is stuck in my throat. I didn't know I was looking like that. Let me go get some water. Matter of fact, I'd rather have something stronger than that."

CHAPTER 16

(Gossip)

Meanwhile, Gregory is at the salon, and is working on a customer's hair. The salon is full, and a customer starts to talk about Courtney while she is waiting for her hair to be done. You know there are always one or two people in a salon, that knows all of the latest gossip. She says, "There's a rumor going around about Courtney, your girl's best friend."

"Who are you talking about? asks Kyra.

"I'm talking about the Diva that comes strutting in here all the time with shades on no matter what time of the year it is. You know the one with the long pretty hair. What's her name?"

"You must be talking about Loving," says Kyra.

"Yea, that's the one," says the woman. "I've been hearing a lot about her so-called friend. She is something else if it is true what is being said. I tell you what. Loving had better watch her back, and get her head out of the clouds, because Courtney is right on her tracks, trying to take over her life," says the woman.

"What do you mean by that? asks Kyra. "That sounds crazy."

"Evidently you must not know much about Courtney. Her mother is a gold digger. She walks around with her nose up in the air, and sleeps with any man that'll give her some money."

"What woman doesn't sleep with men for money? asks another customer.

"Not everybody is like that. I know I'm not."

"Okay ladies, can you get back to the subject about Courtney please?" asks Kyra.

"Oh, okay, well, I heard that she has been seen sneaking over to Loving's boyfriend house a lot lately. I have a friend who doesn't live too far from him. She says that she has been seeing Courtney's car around there quite often."

"I don't believe it," says Gregory.

"I can tell that you and Loving are good friends. You don't believe nothing if it was staring right in your face."

"That's no proof that Courtney's seeing the man behind Loving's back. Courtney and Loving are real tight," says Gregory.

"This should make the hair on your neck stand up. I usually don't get into other people's business like this, but my sister works in a doctor's office, and told me that Courtney was there, and was bragging about being pregnant. Come to find out, she wasn't, and cussed the nurses and doctor out for telling her that she wasn't. She said she was about to call security, for Courtney really acted up in there," says another customer.

"Is she losing her mind or something? asks Kyra.

"Courtney is no more a threat to Loving than a damn fly," says Gregory.

"I don't know Gregory. Maybe you should think about this. Everybody is not going to be bashing Courtney like this. Now, I see if it was Loving that they were talking about, for she has a lot of women who are jealous of her," says Kyra.

"You included," says one of the stylists.

"Shut up! All I know is that Courtney doesn't have anything that a lot of women could be jealous of. You hear what somebody just said, that her mother is a whore and Courtney probably sticks by Loving because she wants to be like Loving. You see she has changed the way she looks now, to look like Loving. Maybe there is some truth to what they are saying."

"You know Loving is my girl. I don't want to go to her and tell her something like this without any proof. I tell you what, when I get out of here, I will definitely go talk to her about this. I know that she is going to tell me to mind my damn business, but I'm going to tell her anyway."

"You better not waste any more time on this. I think that Courtney may be losing her mind," says the woman.

"I wouldn't take it that far," says Gregory.

"Okay, don't say that I didn't tell you first, and warn you about her. The thing about it is I'm not the only one who is noticing this. To tell you the truth, Courtney never did anything to me, so I have nothing against her. I'm trying to tell you something so that you can protect your friend that's all."

"This is getting too damn scary for me. Do you really think that Courtney would try to hurt Loving?" asks Kyra.

"I don't know, but you all have me really thinking now. Anything is possible these days. I tell you what though, if I found out this is true, I will beat her ass myself as much as Loving has helped her out," says Gregory.

CHAPTER 17

(A Strange Feeling)

Back at Maxine's house, Loving's mother Brooke calls, and says that she will be home soon from her cruise, and can't wait to tell them about the trip. That she misses them all, and tells Loving that she loves her and as soon as she gets back home they are going to spend more time together. She knows that they haven't been connecting a lot lately. "I'm so sorry baby for neglecting you so much, but I'm going to make it up to you when I get home tomorrow."

"There's no need for you to be sorry Mom. You have a life to lead too. I'm not a child anymore," says Loving.

"You will always be my baby," says Brooke.

"Where's Dad?" asks Loving.

"He's checking in our bags. I'll tell him that you said hello," says Brooke.

"Tell him that I love him, and can't wait to see him," says Loving.

"I sure will baby. Love you, hugs and kisses," says Brooke.

"Hugs and kisses," says Loving, as she hangs up her phone, not knowing that it will be the last time that they will talk again.

"Look at me getting all syrupy. That's strange, for I've never done that before. I don't know why I'm starting to feel like that now," says Loving.

"Sometimes it's like that sweetie. There's nothing wrong with that. You just miss your Mommy that's all," says Maxine now hugging Loving.

"That's probably what it is. I get like that sometimes about my Mom too," says Courtney.

"You seem to do a lot of things like Loving don't you Courtney?" asks Morgan.

"What do you mean by that?" asks Courtney.

"I saw you the other day with Paige and I was about to get out of my car and come behind you, and grab you. I only saw you from behind, and I'm glad that when you turned around, I realized that you weren't my sister. I would have gotten slapped."

"We were talking about that just before you came in," says Elaine.

"We sure were, it's kind of eerie to me," says Maxine.

"This is being blown all out of proportion," says Loving. I think it's time for us to go anyway. Come on Courtney," says Loving.

"Oh well, I guess you like that kind of stuff," says Morgan.

"Why don't you just mind your business and find you a girlfriend or boyfriend or whatever else floats your damn boat?" asks Loving.

"Why be so sensitive? Unless you have something going on with Courtney, that's why you don't mind her going around looking just like you," says Morgan.

"Hush your mouth. You two stop it this minute. I will not have you two talking like that to each other. I don't ever want to hear you two talk like that against each other again do you hear me?" asks Elaine.

"I apologize for disrespecting you like that Aunt Elaine. It won't happen again," says Loving.

"I'm sorry too. Sorry sis, I didn't mean to come out the mouth like that. Love you," says Morgan as he hugs Loving.

"Love you too," says Loving as she whispers in Morgan's ear, "Say something like that again, and I will tell Gregory about you and Christopher." She smiles at him and walks away as Morgan stands there with a surprised look on his face. "It's time for us to go now. I have another stop to go to, so I will talk to you all later. It's been real."

"Thanks for inviting me," says Courtney.

"Bye big brother," says Loving, as she waves at him while going out the door.

"That is a stone cold bitch right there" he says to himself.

CHAPTER 18

(The Revealing)

"I'm glad to get out of there," says Loving

"Why do you say that? I like your family," says Courtney.

"Sometimes they can get on my last nerve, especially my brother. They always try to get into my business. They had no reason to be saying things about you like that. I wonder what made them change like that anyway. I take it as a compliment that you want to look like me. We are best friends, and best friends sometimes do things that the other one does. I don't see anything wrong with it," says Loving.

"Me neither. Just as you said, we are best friends, and "I think by us being so close, some people don't like that," says Courtney.

"It's a shame that some people are like that, but that's their problem. I don't have time to be worried about what other people think. To hell with them, and who doesn't want to be like Loving?"

"That's right, to hell with them. I think they are jealous of us being so close that's the problem," says Courtney. As they are talking, Loving pulls up beside a car with a man and a woman in it. She looks over into the car and the man is looking at her smiling. She pulls her shades up and winks at the man as she drives off when the light changes. She can hear the woman in the car starting to argue with the man as she is leaving.

"You are bad, you know that?" asks Courtney.

"I was just having a little fun. I don't know why she was so upset over a little flirting," says Loving innocently.

When they arrive at their destination at the mall, lo and behold, there is the couple that she had seen at the light.

"Courtney sees them and says, "Loving, don't look now, but that same couple is behind you," says Courtney as if she is afraid.

"And?" asks Loving, as she switches through the mall in front of them with her short jacket on and skinny jeans. "I'm getting a little thirsty. Let's stop over at the Food Court so that I can get something to drink."

As they are placing their orders, Loving sees some guys sitting at one of the tables watching them. There is one guy who is staring at her, and she blows a kiss at him.

"Bitch!" says a young lady as she walks past them and goes to sit where the guy that was staring at her is sitting.

A woman hears what the young lady calls Loving and asks, "I bet you get that all the time don't you?"

At first Loving doesn't say anything and Courtney answers for her. "Yes she does, all the time."

I want to tell you something that I don't want you to ever forget. If anyone ever calls you a Bitch again, just remember, that a Bitch means a woman who is Being In Total Control of Herself," so just brush it off, and keep on stepping."

"I never heard anything like that before," says Courtney.

"I haven't either, but I tell you what, just like she said, I will never forget it," says Loving.

"Believe me, I've been called that so many times, that it's not even funny. I want you to know that to not make that word make you," says the woman.

"Thank-you," says Loving.

"You're welcome, and watch the company that you keep," says the woman as she walks away.

"That was kind of strange there wasn't it?" asks Courtney.

"There's a lot of strange things in this world. As my Nanna always says, "Nothing is a coincidence in this world. Everything happens for a reason. You just have to read between the lines sometimes to find the answer," says Loving.

CHAPTER 19

(The Last Day)

On the way home from the mall, Loving decides to call Chance to let him know that she will be by there, not telling him that Courtney is with her. He tells her to come on over. The thing is, Courtney doesn't know who Loving is talking to because Loving tells her that she is stopping over someone's house for a minute. When they stop in front of Chance house, Courtney starts to hyperventilate. She starts to breathe really fast, and can't seem to catch her breath.

Loving takes off her seatbelt, and helps Courtney take her seatbelt off. Courtney starts to wave her arms around and then Loving gets out of the car and rushes around to the passenger side where Courtney is sitting. She opens the car door, and helps Courtney out of the car.

"No, no, no!" shouts Courtney, as Loving tries to lead her to the front door of Chance' house.

"Yes, come on, what in the hell is wrong with you? I'm trying to get you some help," says Loving, now getting annoyed by the way Courtney is acting.

When they get to the door, Loving rings the doorbell. In a few minutes, Chance is standing there. Loving doesn't give him a chance to react, and pushes her and Courtney inside.

"What the hell do you think you're doing? I know damn well that you didn't bring this Bitch in my house."

Loving is looking surprised as she helps Courtney onto the sofa.

"What are you talking about? This is Courtney," she states.

"I know damn well who she is. I want this Bitch out of my house right now!" he shouts. While this is going on, Courtney is trying to get up off of the sofa, but Loving is holding her back.

"Wait a minute here. What's going on?" Why are you talking about her like that?" asks Loving surprisingly.

"This tramp that you call a friend has been coming over here letting me fuck her for months now," says Chance.

"He's lying!" He's lying!" shouts Courtney.

"What? I don't think that I heard you right," says Loving.

"Oh you heard me alright. This Bitch here, says that she's pregnant by me," says Chance.

"Pregnant? What? You and Courtney have been fucking each other behind my back? Oh no, this can't be happening," says Loving.

"Yes, your whoring ass so-called best friend has been sucking my penis like a lolli-pop every chance she gets. Even when you were in the hospital, she did it right in the Custodial Room."

"No, I don't believe it. You're just trying to get back at me for something that's all. You're trying to make me jealous that's all," says Loving now crying.

"Hell if I am." You may as well tell the truth, because I told you the next time that I see you, I would kill you and the baby didn't I?"

"Hold up. Is this true Courtney? Please say it's not true," pleads Loving. Courtney is sitting on the sofa rocking back and forth crying.

"Yes, it's true; I did what he said you wouldn't do. I did everything that he said I did and more. I'm so tired of being the second one that men look at. I wanted to see how it feels to be the one that all the men wanted. I did it, and I would do it all over again if I had a chance."

"You Bitch!" shouts Loving, as she runs and jumps on Courtney and they start to fight. Chance pulls them apart, and starts to hit Courtney in her face. He then takes Courtney and swings her across the room. She falls against the wall, and then Chance goes to help Loving up. As he is helping Loving, Courtney runs out to the car and gets her bag and comes back into the house. When she walks in, she takes out a gun that she had purchased after Chance had threatened her the first time for her protection.

"Hold it right there, you no-good bastard."

Chance turns around and sees that Courtney has a gun in her hand pointing it in their direction.

"Whoa, wait a minute now," he says.

"Shut up! You've said enough already, and if you open your damn mouth again, I will put something in there to make sure that you'll never talk again," shouts Courtney.

"Why Courtney?" asks Loving.

"Why Courtney?" mocks Courtney at Loving. Do you really want to know why? I'll tell you why you stupid Bitch. "It's because I wanted to dammit." You know what else? The information I got about you Chance was from Kyra's husband. The dumb bastard thinks I'm in love with him too. Men, you all think with your penis. Not to say that I didn't enjoy it. It was fun. Let's do it again sometimes."

"This is crazy," says Loving.

"You know what's crazy, it's you. You live in this fantasy world where it's all about Loving. Loving this, Loving that. I'm so tired of hearing your name I could scream. Now get on your knees, and beg for your life she tells them.

"What do you want from me?" asks Loving.

"You know what I want from you really?" asks Courtney. "I'll tell you what I want you to do for me before I take your life. I want you to kiss my ass literally."

"What? You're kidding right?" asks Loving.

"We'll see who's kidding. Now get over here and kiss my ass now." Loving gets up off of the sofa and kneels down in front of Courtney.

"Wait a minute. Let me pull my pants down so that you can kiss my naked ass. Courtney turns around so that Loving can kiss her. "If you try anything, I will blow her damn head off," says Courtney to Chance. "Now kiss it Bitch," says Courtney as large drops of tears roll down Loving's face.

"Please don't make me do this," she pleads.

"Didn't I tell you to shut the hell up before? Now, don't make me madder than I already am. This is for all the times that I had to kiss your ass just to be around you. Now kiss it until I tell you to stop."

Loving leans over and kisses Courtney all the while the gun is pointed at her head.

"That's right. Good girl. Just like a good Bitch obeying her master."

"You are a sick woman you know that. As soon as Chance says that, Courtney fires a shot at him and misses. Loving reacts by knocking Courtney down and goes for the gun. This gives Chance time to get up, and they all wrestle with the gun. Courtney's pants are still down at her ankles so she is tangled, but still has a firm grasp on the gun.

When Loving gets up from the floor and tries to run to call for help, the gun goes off again, and she is hit in the back. She falls to the floor and Chance then takes the gun away from Courtney and shoots her with it. He rushes to call 911, and then checks to see how Loving is doing.

"Hang in there baby. Everything is going to be alright."

THE END

I hope that you all have enjoyed reading this novel as much as I have enjoyed writing it for you. Even though this is a fictional story, incidents like this happen everyday. Boys who witness, or who are victims themselves of domestic violence, are twice as likely to abuse their partners and children when they become adults. Many teen girls and women do not report domestic violence, because they feel it is a private matter, and feel that their male partner will change. If you or someone you know are being abused, please get help as soon as possible. Call the National Domestic Violence Hotline. 1-800-799-SAFE-(7233)

Ms. Penny Glover, is a writer she has won many awards, which includes poetry. She has been nominated for, "Who's Who of the East", The Larry Neal Award, and the D.C. Mayors Arts Award for her first novel, "It Hurts When Love Dies." Ms Glover is a native Washingtonian.